CANDLELIGHT REGENCY SPECIAL

CANDLELIGHT ROMANCES

174 The Moonlight Gondola, JANETTE RADCLIFFE
173 Serena, JACQUELYN AEBY
175 The Encounter, RUTH MC CARTHY SEARS
176 Diary of Danger, JACQUELYN AEBY
178 House of the Sphinx, LOUISE BERGSTROM
177 The Trillium Cup, JACQUELYN AEBY
180 The Secret of the Priory, SOFI O'BRYAN
181 Wait for Love, ARLENE HALE
179 Bride of Belvale, HARRIET RICH
182 Dangerous Assignment, JENNIFER BLAIR
183 Walk a Dark Road, LYNN WILLIAMS
184 Counterfeit Love, JACQUELYN AEBY
185 The Gentleman Pirate, JANETTE RADCLIFFE
187 Tower in the Forest, ETHEL HAMILL
186 The Golden Falcon, BETTY HALE HYATT
188 Master of Roxton, ELISABETH BARR
189 The Steady Flame, BETH MYERS
191 Cottage on Catherina Cay, JACQUELYN AEBY
190 White Jasmine, JANETTE RADCLIFFE
192 Quest for Alexis, NANCY BUCKINGHAM
193 Falconer's Hall, JACQUELYN AEBY
195 The Long Shadow, JENNIFER BLAIR
194 Shadows of Amanda, HELEN S. NUELLE
197 A Dream of Her Own, MARYANN YOUNG
196 Portrait of Errin, BETTY HALE HYATT
199 The Storm, JACQUELYN AEBY
198 Lord Stephen's Lady, JANETTE RADCLIFFE
200 Dr. Myra Comes Home, ARLENE HALE
201 Winter in a Dark Land, MIRIAM LYNCH
203 A Happy Ending, ARLENE HALE
202 The Sign of the Blue Dragon, JACQUELYN AEBY
204 The Azure Castle, JANETTE RADCLIFFE
205 Never Look Back, JACQUELYN AEBY
206 The Topaz Charm, JANETTE RADCLIFFE
207 Teach Me to Love, GAIL EVERETT
209 Share Your Heart, ARLENE HALE
208 The Brigand's Bride, BETTY HALE HYATT
210 The Gallant Spy, BETTY HALE HYATT
211 Love Is the Winner, GAIL EVERETT
212 Scarlet Secrets, JANETTE RADCLIFFE
213 Revelry Manor, ELISABETH BARR
214 Pandora's Box, BETTY HALE HYATT
215 Safe Harbor, JENNIFER BLAIR

A GIFT OF VIOLETS

Janette Radcliffe

A CANDLELIGHT REGENCY SPECIAL

Published by
Dell Publishing Co., Inc.
1 Dag Hammarskjold Plaza
New York, New York 10017

ISBN: 0-440-12891-9

Printed in the United States of America
First printing—March 1977
Second printing—April 1977
Third printing—May 1978

CHAPTER 1

The air of Florence felt warm after the chill of the British winter, and the garden was radiant with flowers. Viola Marchmont, enchanted, bent again and again to gather a spray of violets, or purple pansies, or the sweet wild pinks.

She carefully placed each spray in the curved basket on her left arm, then straightened again to gaze at the intense blue of the Italian sky, with puffy white clouds drifting like baby hair across to the gaunt hills. The buildings about her, of gray stone or red brick, with red or green tiled roofs, were hundreds of years old. All was as she had seen in paintings, even to the features of the Italians who walked past the low stone walls of the gardens. One girl, with her long brown curls, her classic features, could have posed for Fra Angelico or Botticelli. Perhaps an ancestor of hers had done so.

Viola drew a deep, happy breath. She was so glad her father had allowed the girls to come with him on this trip. Florence, after the brutal wars of the Napoleonic times, was settling down to peace once more, under the reign of the Grand Duke Ferdinand III of Tuscany. In April 1818, life seemed gentle and serene in the old city.

Her father, Sir Anthony, was on a diplomatic mission, and would remain in Florence at least six months. It was worth renting a villa, and setting up to entertain, with Viola's eldest sister, Eleanor, acting as hostess, and Bernice to attract any man in sight with her sleek beauty. Viola was happy to take care of the beautiful home for them, to soothe the servants in her newly acquired Italian, to do some of the marketing, and to arrange the flowers.

Her sisters were out this morning, paying a call on the Russian ladies who had arrived a month ago. When would they consider Viola old enough to accompany them? she wondered with a little frown marring her smooth young forehead. Their mother had died ten years ago, and Eleanor had assumed control of her youngest sister. Now Eleanor and Bernice had been presented in society, attended balls frequently, sipped tea in elegant company—but Viola still felt confined to the nursery.

Well—maybe when she was eighteen, she thought. But that would be almost another year! And she did so long to dance, and gaze at the marvelous costumes of the ladies of society, and hear the social chitchat.

Her father was working, shut in his study alone for a change. Something was troubling him, she thought, her gaze fixed on the distant hills. She was sensitive to him; she could know his moods when Eleanor was imperiously demanding, or Bernice sweetly murmuring for what she wished. Something about returning to Florence—it held memories for him, after all. He had been here for quite a time during the wars, but he would never discuss it. Of course, he was a diplomat, and he rarely discussed anything about his work.

She held a spray of violets to her chin, musingly, then dipped her small nose into their fragrance happily, and turned back to the villa, golden in its green setting of hedges and cypresses. It was then she saw the man at the low wall.

Viola stared at him. From a distance, he looked like many of the Italians she had noticed on the streets of Florence—tall, slim, with black curly hair, and a profile like those on coins. But as she came closer—for he waited as though to speak to her—she was shocked to see that his tanned face was marred by the dull red of a brutal scar, which streaked across the beautiful profile.

She could not guess his age. The scar had blurred him to everyman, stoical, patient, hard, and his gaze was keen on her as she approached. She could not stare at his face.

When she was about ten feet from him, he spoke. "*Ma donna*, you belong to this villa, *si*?"

"Yes, I belong here," she said gently, then switched to her halting Italian. "You wish to see someone here, *signore*?"

He replied in Italian then, slowly, as though measuring his words to her understanding. "I wish to see the gentleman of the villa, Sir Anthony Marchmont. He is at home?"

She hesitated. He was well-dressed, in a black suit of good material and a white ruffled shirt with lace at the cuffs. And on one hand was a crested ring, a strange figure in gold on a purple setting. He could scarcely be applying for work.

Perhaps he was someone connected with her father's mission here. She wished Hector McIntyre, her father's aide, were about; he was so sensible and helpful. But he had escorted the sisters to tea today, as her father had wished.

"He is at home. Please come around to the door and someone will open it to you. I will see if Father can talk to you now."

She hastened to the inner door of the villa, as the man went around the wall. She was in the hallway in time to see the butler open the door to him. She gave him a smile, and nodded to the butler, then hurried to the door of her father's study. Only then did she realize that she had neglected to obtain the man's name.

She tapped lightly, and entered the massive study. Her father's graying brown head was bent over the papers spread out on a huge mahogany desk. He raised it impatiently, his blue eyes glazed with thought.

"Father, excuse me for interrupting you. There is a gentleman to see you."

"What name?" snapped her father. "I am busy this morning."

Behind her, the man entered quietly. Her father stared, about to say something rude, then rose slowly, gripping his pen as though it were a weapon. "My God—" he choked.

The man bowed. Viola had turned, and thought his face was mocking. "Even so. It is I, Sir Anthony."

"I thought you were dead!" Sir Anthony blurted, his poise badly shaken.

"Not I. Only my entire family—my parents, my sister, my cousins, my nephew," said the man, as though reciting a lesson carefully learned.

Viola gasped, clutching her basket of flowers to her.

The man did not turn his head; his gaze rested intently on her father.

"Close the door, Viola," her father snapped.

"Shall–shall I go?" she whispered.

At last the man turned toward her, the brown eyes so full of emotion that they seemed black. "No, remain, *signorina.* I wish you to understand why I am here, why I speak to your father, the good Sir Anthony."

There was a sneer in his voice and his face. Viola went to the door, wishing she could run away. She felt a cold certainty that she did not want to hear the words that would follow. She closed the door, though, and set her basket on a table near it. The Italian was courteously holding a straight-back chair for her, and waved her to it, then took another chair for himself, in a leisurely manner.

Sir Anthony sank back into his armchair. Viola thought his hands shook, although his face was again schooled to cool politeness.

"How did you get away?" Sir Anthony's gaze could not seem to move away from the scarred cheek. The man shrugged, his palms lifted. His hands too were scarred, Viola saw, great furrows ran along the palms and the back of his hands, into the lace ruffles of his sleeves.

"That is no matter. Another story for another time," he was saying in English. "You will introduce me, perhaps?"

Sir Anthony gathered his wits. "Viola, this is–Giorgio Michieli. I–knew him in the late wars, *Signor* Michieli, my youngest daughter, Viola."

The man rose, bowed to her, and sat down again. The formalities over, he seemed to forget her as she sat quietly in her chair, her hands clasped tightly in the lap of violet muslin. Drums seemed to beat in her ears, and she felt slightly sick. He had said his entire family was dead. How? When?

"I learned a month ago that you were returning to Florence. The news was of great interest to me, Sir Anthony. I had not thought you would dare return."

Her father's shoulders straightened. "Dare? An odd word to use," he said with his usual crispness. "I did my duty, as we all did. Once Napoleon was defeated, I resigned from the service. However, I was called back on a special mission."

"Florentines have long memories, sir. However, you did not expect me to remain alive to have a memory. Eh?"

"No, I did not expect it. May I say—I am extremely happy that you escaped that trap—"

"The trap of your planning, *signore.*" The quiet voice was more deadly now. "Yes, I escaped it. However, my parents did not. My sister endured three days and nights of torture before she escaped into death. The fiends used her—ah, but I shall not speak of it before your daughter. She is young and tender, eh?"

Sir Anthony put his hand to his face. His forehead was wet with perspiration. "I never dreamed they would—my God," he groaned. "It was a chance we all took, of being betrayed—"

"But not by an ally, *signore,*" the merciless soft voice continued. "No, I did not expect it of you. One lives and learns, eh?"

Viola was trembling. The soft voice, speaking such terrible things . . . was she in a nightmare? His own sister, used by vile men—tortured—and he himself with those horrible scars.

"Did you—tell them what they wanted to know?" Sir Anthony seemed to force himself to speak.

The lean shoulders, powerful inside the well-tailored coat raised in a shrug. "No, I did not," he said flatly. "But that is five years ago. It is over."

"What do you want of me, then?" Sir Anthony asked after a pause. He was unusually pale, and his long fingers drummed on the desk. "You did not come to renew our acquaintance, I presume?"

"You are perceptive, as always," the man said, without a smile. "No, I come to accuse you of the deaths of my family, my parents, my sister, everyone. You betrayed them to the enemy. You knew it when you sent me on that mission."

"I thought it would be dangerous, yes," Sir Anthony admitted, in a low tone. "We all knew the chance you took. You knew it yourself."

"I was captured before I left the city," the man said flatly. "Someone betrayed me. Someone—and only you knew of the plan." The man leaned forward, as though hopefully, but Sir Anthony shook his head.

"I can only say—how sorry I am. It was not intentional. When I heard you were caught, I could only hope for a quick death for you."

Giorgio Michieli leaned back with a faint sigh. "Thank you, of course," he said ironically. "But as you see, I am not dead. I am alive, and yearning these years for vengeance."

The word seemed to hiss in the room, as cold water into a flame. Vengeance. The revenge of an Italian, a Florentine. Viola had heard of families here who carried their hatred through centuries.

She made some involuntary sound, and the man turned to her with the litheness of a black panther. "And you, *Signorina* Viola, what do you imagine would repay me for what I have suffered and lost? What would replace the loss of my family? Eh?"

She answered quietly, though her heart pounded like thunder. "Nothing could replace them, nothing. I am so sorry, *signore*. It is a terrible thing to have happened to you. You—you must be a man of much—courage," she added in a low tone.

The dark eyes flicked over her; she did not know what he was thinking. Sir Anthony stirred uneasily, then finally asked, "Were you thinking of money? Do you want money from me? I can pay you. I imagine you lost most of your possessions in the late wars. Do you wish to name a price?"

"Oh, Father!" whispered Viola, deeply shocked.

He waved an impatient hand at her. "Stay out of this, if you please! You are too young to understand. I should not have allowed you to remain."

She clenched her fists. "To speak of money, when he has lost everything!"

Giorgio's cool tone interrupted. "Money is a soothing balm, *signorina*. Do not despise it. With money, a man may do much. I will consider the matter, and let you know. There is a price for everything in this world, as you will know when you are older."

He rose, and so did Sir Anthony, rather pale but composed. "I shall come again tomorrow at this time," he said. "I shall consider what my price will be. Until tomorrow." And he bowed, and went to the door.

Viola followed him slowly. "Viola, we have guests for lunch, be sure all is ready," her father said sharply. "One o'clock. Your sisters should return soon. Send Eleanor to me, and say nothing of this matter to anyone, do you hear?"

"Yes, Father."

Giorgio Michieli opened the door for her, and she

went out. He lifted the basket from the table, and followed her. "Your flowers, *Signorina* Viola." He handed them to her, then hesitated, gazing down at her. "Of what age are you?" he asked.

"Seventeen," she replied.

He nodded, his eyes unexpectedly full of pain. "The age of my young sister, when she–" He did not finish his sentence, but went to the door, and the butler bowed him out. Viola stood in the cool, dim hallway, her heart so full of suffering for him that she could scarcely endure it. The scar on his face was echoed by deeper scars on his mind and his soul.

She was busy then until luncheon. There were the flowers to arrange, the table to supervise. She went to the kitchen to make sure the Italian chef had all in readiness. The salads were not prepared, and to the chef's horror, she put on an apron and began to cut and trim the vegetables.

Carmela Pisani found her there. The pleasant spinster of about thirty, who had been hired as Viola's maid, had promptly made herself confidante, duenna, and adviser as well. "But little Viola, you do not do this," she said, outraged. She and the chef began an argument in Italian, which Viola halted.

"I am accustomed to this, please do not argue. I enjoy cooking and arranging the table." She gave them a dimpled smile, mischief in her gray eyes, and they melted.

The chef patted her hand. "Such a clever little lady, and not yet married. She will be a fine wife to some fortunate man."

"He had best appreciate her, or he will have me to answer to," said Carmela grandly.

Viola laughed at them both. Later in the dining room, as she sat demurely at the center of the table, listening to her sister Eleanor drawling in her clever fashion, Viola thought, "It will be years, if ever, before anyone will want to marry me. Bernice, yes, she is so beautiful and charms everyone, like a cat who is accustomed to cream. And Eleanor, some diplomat will snap her up, she is so intelligent and polished and clever. But they do not even look at me!"

And it was true. Their guests were all in the diplomatic corps. Hector McIntyre, her father's present aide, was an ambitious Scotchman, red-haired and ruddy of complexion. Amiable and anxious to please, he silently adored Eleanor. He was always kind to Viola, but he did not really see her, she thought.

Reginald Selby had been an aide to Sir Anthony during the late wars. At the moment, he was conversing with Eleanor, leaning to catch her least word. With his straight blond hair and shrewd green eyes, he was indisputably handsome. Her father seemed fond of him, and Eleanor was attracted; Viola knew by the softening of her elder sister's sharp gray eyes, and by the flirtatious way she held her head. She was wearing her cream and gold dress this noon. Mr. Selby was divorced, and there had been a scandal over it, so said Carmela, who had pursed her lips disapprovingly. But this hint of trouble over women made Eleanor more intrigued. She said she had never liked the easy conquests.

And then there was Niccolo Leopardo. When Selby was placed at Eleanor's right, Leonardo had been inclined to pout. But Bernice, next to him, was coaxing him back to good humor in her irresistible fashion; her blue eyes gazed intently into his small black ones. He was not a favorite of Viola's; in fact, she had taken a dislike to him. He was a widower of some forty years, with no children, and a frank interest in remarrying. He had played some part in Sir Anthony's activities five years ago, and was clearly delighted to meet with him again, or so he said.

The rest of the table was made up of two Italian couples, of which the wives did not speak English. Viola talked to them in her still-halting Italian, which made them smile with pleasure.

The luncheon was leisurely, prolonged as it was often in the Marchmont household. Sir Anthony did much of his work, he often said to the girls, surrounded by the pleasures of the dining table. Good wine, delicious food, and brandy to follow, made mellow the toughest of diplomats.

Viola's thoughts wandered today, as the courses followed each other. She was alert to the serving—she must train one of the footmen again, she reminded herself. He was young and nervous, but had promise, and was willing to learn. The soup course was followed by pasta with meat and cream sauce. Bernice frowned over it, and ate only a little. She was inclined to fat, Viola knew. But the men ate heartily.

Viola had planned a veal course to follow, with salad, and then cheese and fruit, in the Italian manner. Since most of the guests were Italian, she sought to please them. Coffee was then served in the drawing room, with brandy for the men who wished it.

It was midafternoon before the guests removed there. Sir Anthony was deep in discussion of Italian politics with one of his more knowledgeable guests. Eleanor was being charming to Reginald Selby and Niccolo Leopardo, in her experienced fashion. Viola slipped away to the kitchen, complimented the chef and his assistants, then ordered more coffee to be served to the ladies.

It was five o'clock before all the guests left, and Viola could relax. Her sisters were lying down in their bedchambers, draperies drawn, pads over their eyes. They were to attend a dance that evening at the home of the British diplomats. Viola had not been invited. Eleanor said positively that she was still too young.

Viola went to her own bedroom to rest. Carmela came to her and insisted on her changing to a light dressing gown and lying down for a while. But she could not sleep. Behind her closed lids was etched the image of the scarred man. She could not forget him, the bitterness of his soft polite tones, the deep grooves on his face and hands.

What price could repay him for what he had suffered, and continued to suffer? She longed to be present when her father met with him again the next morning. She wished she had been clever in saying something to him, something that might help take away the bitterness of the years. But such remarks seemed beyond her. His entire family, wiped away in such a horrible fashion! How he must have ached with bitterness and grief, what hatred he must feel even now.

CHAPTER 2

Viola went down to breakfast early the next morning, hoping to find her father alone. Her sisters usually slept late, especially after a dance. Her hopes were rewarded when she found Sir Anthony frowning over a letter, his coffee neglected at his side.

She came over to him, kissed the cheek offered to her, and took her place beside him. She motioned to the footman to replace his cold coffee with hot, and added cream and sugar, as he liked. Then she accepted her own plate from the servant.

Sir Anthony laid down the letter with a sigh. She wondered if it might be a good time to ask to be present at the next meeting with the scarred man. But her father spoke abruptly.

"*Signor* Michieli writes to say he cannot come this morning. He will come tomorrow afternoon at four. He wishes all three of my daughters to be present."

Viola widened her eyes at him. "Oh—really?" She

was disappointed. She guessed the man would not speak freely with all of them there.

"I wish I knew what was in his mind." Sir Anthony waved the footman away. When they were alone in the room, he said, "Giorgio was always shrewd beyond his years. A clever and deep man. There is something about this—"

"What—what vengeance do you think he wishes?" asked Viola in a low tone.

Sir Anthony shrugged, sipping at his coffee. "Heaven knows. You have said nothing to your sisters?"

"No, of course not."

He sighed again. "I must speak to them today, so they comprehend the situation. I am in no position to refuse him whatever he asks. Fortunately, my financial situation is good. I can pay anything, within reason. Odd—he never seemed to think much of money, but of course his family was formerly wealthy. Had a villa up in the hills near Fiesole, and a house in Rome. He probably lost everything, poor chap."

"He lost his family," Viola reminded him. She set down her fork. She had lost her appetite. She could not forget his face when he had spoken of his sister.

"Yes. He was extremely fond of them all, very proud of them. Close family ties, these Italians. Came from a long line, several centuries old. I suppose he must be very bitter. He used to be a fine chap, do anything for one. Loyal as they come. I counted on his honesty and integrity. And he seemed to like and trust me."

Viola bit back harsh words. Sir Anthony would not willingly have betrayed anyone, she thought anxiously. There must be some story behind this. Her father was just and honorable. What could have happened?

Sir Anthony rose abruptly. "Well, since he is not coming this morning, I'll go out and see a chap I must speak to. I will return for luncheon before one. You recall we have dinner guests. They will arrive about eight."

"Yes, Father. The family you spoke of, and others—I have the names."

"Good girl." He patted her shoulder absently.

"Father? Could—could I go into Florence? I must do a little shopping. Will you need the small carriage?"

"Um—no. I'll ride. But take Carmela with you. Never go alone into the city, Viola," he said severely. "You tend to be too trusting. Take Carmela, and have Bernardo drive you. I trust him."

"Thank you, Father," she said gratefully. She left her breakfast and sped to her bedroom, then rang for Carmela. They would be off and away before her sisters awoke and thought of little duties for her, such as ironing their ruffles and dressing their hair. She did not resent it, but it did take so much time. She longed to explore Florence, but her sisters thought that a waste of time. Who wanted to look at old buildings and strange statues?

"Father said I might take the small carriage, Carmela," she told her maid gleefully as soon as the woman arrived. "Hurry! Tell Bernardo he is to drive us, and we'll escape!"

"Escape, *signorina*?" Carmela looked scandalized.

"I mean, we will go out shopping and looking, and we might have tea in one of those little outdoor cafés."

"Oh, *si, si, si*!" And Carmela scurried off in her loose slippers, beaming at the thought.

Viola swiftly brushed her hair into neat curls about her face, and pinched her cheeks to make them more pink. Eleanor did not approve of makeup for her youngest sister. She put on her ruffled bonnet, tied the ribbons neatly, frowned at her simple blue muslin gown, and set the matching pelisse about her shoulders. Eleanor's new dresses had five rows of ruffles about the hem. Viola's had only a simple embroidered design of scrolling. She sighed. When would they allow her to look grown-up and fashionable?

Carmela returned, neat and stern-looking, belying her excitement. She had donned a black serge costume with a wide white lace ruffle about the throat and a dark coat to match. They hurried out to the carriage, where Bernardo greeted them with a doffing of his cap and a broad grin. He was already fond of the little blond *signorina* who troubled to speak Italian to him. Those others, they lifted their chins and scolded him in English very fast, so that he could not understand a word they said.

Carmela had been assigned to be Eleanor's maid, but Eleanor had refused to have an Italian, and pouted until Sir Anthony had found an English maid, who waited on both her and Bernice. Viola much preferred Carmela, and the older woman seemed fond of her also. Viola settled her blue skirts in the small carriage, and nodded to Bernardo.

"First the shops near the cathedral," she directed, and they were off. She quickly found the white gloves and ribbons her sisters wanted, and dared to buy some long gloves for herself in blue and violet. Then they left Bernardo to wait for them while they walked about the cathedral, admiring the fine marble work of the exterior, the delicate seashell coloring of Giotto's tower. The elegance of the tower had drawn Viola's admiration from the first, and she sighed with delight as they walked around the side and gazed up at it. How soft the colors, how airy the open windows, how graceful the soaring against the blue sky.

Inside the cathedral, they paused again and again at the altars, and Viola and Carmela knelt at the foot of their favorite Virgin. Today Viola did not think of her family. Her thoughts and prayers were all for the scarred man. She murmured, "Let him find peace and even joy once more. Wipe out the bitterness from his heart, so he might truly live in light and hope again." Although Viola was not a Catholic, she found unusual serenity in this cathedral, and especially before this chosen statue.

She felt strangely better about Giorgio Michieli when they left the cathedral. It was growing late. They had some tea at a café, where Viola mused over her own thoughts, and Carmela scowled disapprovingly at any men who dared to gaze boldly at her pretty blond *signorina*. No one came close—they did not dare, with Carmela sitting erect as a black cane at her side, and Bernardo gazing warningly from the carriage.

They returned at twelve-thirty, and Viola hurried to her room, washed, and rushed to the kitchen. The chef had all in readiness. Eleanor came to her plaintively.

"Where have you been, Viola? The maid has not done my hair as I wished."

"But it looks beautiful, so charming and soft," said Viola truthfully. "You will have *Signor* Martelli at your right hand, will you not? He longs to talk with you."

Eleanor's mind was distracted from her hair, and she graciously consented to do her best with the difficult man. "But that is tonight," she said. "Who is coming for luncheon?"

"Only Father, he said. He—he wishes to speak with us all," said Viola. Eleanor was curious as a cat, but Viola only shook her head at her sister's questions, and asked her to wait.

Sir Anthony returned wearily at one o'clock, and the girls tactfully allowed him to relax over his luncheon before speaking seriously. Finally Viola motioned for the footman to serve coffee, then leave them.

When the door was closed, she gazed at her father thoughtfully. Were the lines in his face deeper than yesterday? Had he lain awake at night? There were dark smudges under his blue eyes. He brushed back his smartly fashioned graying brown hair, and began.

"My daughters, a man is coming to tea this afternoon. I have deliberately invited him alone. You will be ready at four o'clock, in your loveliest gowns, and I wish you all to be most gracious to him."

"What man, Father?" Bernice murmured eagerly. "An Italian, someone wealthy? Are you matchmaking, Father?"

"No, of course not!" he snapped, and Bernice blinked at him in surprise. He rarely adopted that tone with her. "He is—an associate of mine in the late wars."

"Oh, the wars. I weary of the late wars," Eleanor said languidly. "All some men can talk of is war, war—"

Sir Anthony shot his eldest daughter a cold look, which she did not notice, for she was busily peeling an orange. "This situation is quite different," he said sternly. "The man is named Giorgio Michieli. He was formerly of a wealthy family here in Florence, one of a long line. Now he is the last member of the family. He was–associated with me in the wars. He–rightly, I fear–blames me for a mission which I suggested. It went wrong–and he was captured and tortured. His entire family was also captured, and all died but him. I still do not know how he escaped."

He paused to take out his handkerchief and wipe his forehead. The two older girls stared at him wide-eyed, silenced for once.

"But surely it was not your fault, Father?" Viola ventured to say. "Someone must have betrayed him, someone who knew–"

He gave her a hard look. "Say nothing more, Viola. You do not know the circumstances. Yes, I think I was to blame. And he is asking for vengeance."

"Vengeance?" Eleanor gasped. "What–what kind? Surely not your life, Papa!" At the horror in her tone, the anguished gesture of her graceful hand reached out to him, his face softened. Eleanor was his favorite, clever and witty, the one most like him.

"I do not think so, Eleanor. All I ask is that you be present at tea, that you not be shocked at anything he says, and allow me to soothe him as best I can. Viola, you have ordered tea and coffee, and–"

"Yes, Father, I will take care of all that." She resolved to make some cakes herself, some sweet ones with the whipped cream which was so abundant here, and the new little wild strawberries, and perhaps some shortbread.

"Good. I depend on you all." He abruptly left the table for the study. The girls were silent until Viola also left and went to the kitchen.

She spent the next two hours making cakes, ordering the best china and silver, arranging flowers in the drawing room, and preparing a fire there. It was a chilly day, and a crackling fire always looked friendly. She had a footman rearrange the furniture so that large armchairs were drawn about the coffee table, and the sofa came forward from its usual stiff place near the wall.

She rushed to change to a dress of violet, and soft silk slippers, also of violet, which tied about her slim ankles. He would probably not even see her with the others girls in the room, but she wished to look her finest for him. About her throat she fastened the small strand of pearls which had been her father's first gift to her mother. The other girls preferred the long strands or the diamonds.

She was alone in the drawing room, standing before the fire, when the butler showed *Signor* Michieli in. He paused at the door, then came forward. She smiled at him timidly and held out her hand. To her surprise, he raised it briefly to his lips, and she felt the warmth of his mouth on her fingers before he let it go.

"*Signorina* Viola," he murmured.

"Good afternoon, *Signor* Michieli. Father will come at once," she said, and sent the butler for him. Sir Anthony hurried from his study, fine in his ruby velvet jacket and gray trousers, a ruby stud in his immaculate white neckcloth.

As they greeted each other, Viola studied *Signor* Michieli furtively. Today he wore a light cream suit with a white neckcloth. In the folds of the cloth was a strange device, the one she had noted on his ring. She saw now that it was a golden sea-dragon on a background of purple enamel. Perhaps a family crest? His keen eyes noted her interest.

"You have observed my crest, *signorina*?" His voice was always soft and deliberate, the accented English precise.

"Yes, I noticed your ring yesterday. What is the device, sir?"

"The sea dragon, which is a favorite of the people of Tuscany. We have—we had such a crest on the door handles of our villa, also above the doorway in stucco, and in many other molds."

"But we are not close to the sea here in Florence, are we?" Her smooth forehead puckered in thought.

"No, *ma donna*," he said. "However, those of Tuscany are frequently descendants of the early Etruscans, and we believe they came from the sea—by way of the sea, that is—from some ancient lands. The sea god Neptune drew them."

She would have questioned him eagerly, but her sisters made their entrance then, and his whole attention was at once given to them. She did not blame him, and with a sigh she turned to her seat at the coffee table. Eleanor was radiant in gold tissue silk, her dark hair smoothly swathed about her face, her white skin like a camellia. Golden earrings swung from her delicate ears.

Bernice was in her favorite blue-green, her dark blond hair in delicate curls about her pointed, catlike face, her blue eyes wide and more innocent with the skillful use of paint. Giorgio Michieli looked from one to the other of them, as though he could not believe in such elegance, such grace, such beauty.

Sir Anthony seemed content to have his daughters draw the guest into light, frothy conversation, charming him, though their eyes darted nervously away from the scarred face. When Eleanor handed his coffee cup to him, and his scarred hand touched her long graceful fingers, she jumped visibly. His gaze hardened.

"Oh, Viola, why did you have to make these strawberry cakes? You know I cannot resist them." Bernice reached greedily for another, pouting as she did so.

Giorgio Michieli was quick to hear. "You prepared these cakes, *ma donna*?" he asked Viola.

"Yes, sir, I enjoy cooking, and—and arranging flowers, and all that," she murmured.

"She is not yet out," said Eleanor firmly. "She has not been presented at court, so she does not attend evening events. Therefore, she has time to see to the housekeeping, which she enjoys."

"I understand," said the man gravely. "She is—what—fifteen, as yet?"

Viola gave him a wide look from her gray eyes. He knew her age! He had asked her yesterday.

"No, she is seventeen," Eleanor said impatiently. "But that is considered quite young in England."

"And two such charming sisters are enough for any company, without adding the—ah—competition of a third beauty? I quite understand," he said without a smile.

Bernice bristled, and Eleanor raised her chin. "I do not understand you, sir," she said haughtily, a flush on her cheeks.

"No matter," he said. He turned to Sir Anthony. "You have spoken to your daughters regarding my—ah—cause?"

The atmosphere in the room quickly changed from heated anger to a sharp chill. Sir Anthony looked abruptly more gray, his face drawn in aging lines.

"Yes, I told them a little of the matter, *signore*," he said. "You seek revenge for a matter of some five years ago. I have told them you wish a price for what happened to you, and to your family."

"Ah, yes. I have been considering that price." Giorgio Michieli gazed down at the blue and rose china in his hand, then set it decisively on a table beside him, his scarred fingers gracefully careful. His tanned face was grim, and the long red scar seemed to stand out more distinctly in the firelight which flickered over his lean form. "*Signorina*, as the eldest, what do you think should be my price for what occurred?"

The usually poised Eleanor visibly shrank from the question, and looked anxiously toward her father, who did not return her gaze. "Why—why, how could I say? Perhaps a—a sum of—fifty thousand pounds?"

Viola swallowed, and could not look at her sister. She thought in the same terms as her father—money! As though any sum in the world could repay such a loss.

The man turned deliberately to Bernice, when Eleanor seemed unable to say more.

"And you, *Signorina* Bernice? What kind of payment would you say?"

Bernice stirred, stretching her legs to the fire. Her green slippers showed, and the slim ankles. "Oh, I should want a home again," she said, with unusual decisiveness. "I should want a villa, and furniture, and money as well. Enough to live in luxury."

He seemed interested in her answer, then as she paused, he turned to Viola. "And you, *ma donna*?" he asked softly. "What price revenge?"

She looked steadily back at him, at the dark eyes, and saw pain and bitterness in them, rigid control in the scarred face, loneliness. "For you, *signore*, I would wish—release from pain, to feel joy again, and happiness," she said steadily. "I have prayed that you would find it."

He turned from her abruptly so that she was at once embarrassed, especially as Eleanor raised her eyebrows at her youngest sister, and Sir Anthony gave her a long, stern look.

"I have been considering the matter carefully," Giorgio Michieli said. "You, Sir Anthony, did me a grave wrong. You have three lovely daughters, fine homes, luxury. It is only right that you share some of this wealth with me, whom you deprived."

Sir Anthony's mouth tightened, but he did not speak. After a long pause, the man went on. "So I have decided. I shall take one of your daughters to wed. I am ugly now, I no longer attract the ladies," and he gave Eleanor a hard, knowing look.

Eleanor clasped her hand about her throat, and Bernice gasped. Only Viola was still, carefully pouring more coffee into her father's cup.

"I am not much in company in Florence," continued the soft, merciless voice. "I have thought to marry, but have met no lady on whom I wish to bestow my name of long lineage. Those to whom I might be attracted are repelled by my face. Those who might endure my face turn away from my—lack of visible assets, such as jewels, furs, and so on. Therefore, Sir Anthony, I shall consider the matter, and choose one of your daughters. They are all beautiful, gracious, well-mannered. I shall court them all. When I have chosen my wife, I shall also expect a large dowry to be provided—say, one hundred thousand pounds, settled on her for life."

He paused. Sir Anthony seemed about to speak. The girls were too horrified to protest.

"In advance," continued the man gently. "I shall

decide soon. You will arrange to have the money paid." He stood up. Sir Anthony stood also, mechanically, his tanned face almost greenish with shock.

The visitor said no more. Sir Anthony accompanied him to the door. Eleanor sat quite still, her hand still clutching her throat, her face quite pale, her eyes stricken. Bernice curled up in her place on the sofa, shuddering, her hands over her eyes. Viola merely gazed at the fire.

Suddenly Sir Anthony appeared in the doorway. "You will say nothing of this to anyone," he said harshly. "I will be in my study."

He departed again, and the door slammed after him. Bernice burst into tears and hurried to her bedroom. Eleanor seemed to be in a daze.

The evening was terrible. The girls were visibly upset; only Viola felt any degree of calm. He would not choose her, but she longed for him to find some comfort. Perhaps he had been wiser than he knew. If he had a family of his own—a wife, eventually children—he might again find the peace of mind he longed for, despite the bitterness that determined his present behavior.

After the guests had left, Bernice and Eleanor argued with their father. Bernice wept openly, and Eleanor was close to tears. Viola listened to their impassioned protests in silence.

"We cannot endure this," cried Eleanor. "He is hard and cruel. What kind of life would he give to his wife? He means to torture the woman! I will not stand for it! This is not the Dark Ages!"

"Enough of this," said Sir Anthony sternly, his face very weary. "He is an honorable man. He would not torture his wife, do not even suggest such a thing! He is a gentleman and was a close associate of mine. I would trust him with my life. It is only a shame that he had to trust me with his! How can I repay him? If only he had asked for money!"

"You are not going to agree to this!" cried Bernice, horrified. "To live with a man of such scars—and in poverty!"

"Not in poverty, with one hundred thousand pounds as dowry," her father replied, with grim humor. "Oh, he knows what he is about. I would settle that on each one of you upon marriage, anyway. And you will have as fine a life as he can afford. He is—or was—gentle and kind."

When they saw he would not be moved, the two older girls retired to Eleanor's room to discuss this calamity. Viola retired, with her usual kiss on her father's cheek. He patted her hand absently.

The next day, the butler brought in large baskets of flowers from *Signor* Michieli. Each was accompanied by a card that bore his crest of a sea dragon. For Eleanor, there were camellias, exquisite, white, with ribbons of gold. For Bernice, he sent red roses, with a blue ribbon. Viola received a smaller basket than the others. In it were lavish Parma violets, fragrant and sweet, and the ribbon was lilac.

"Well, he makes a pretty gesture," Eleanor said graciously, gathering up her camellias.

Bernice sniffed. Viola took her violets to her room, and arranged them in a delft china bowl of blue and white. She hovered over them, and gazed at the card soberly. His name was engraved on it. She studied the graceful little sea dragon, and finally turned over the card. She had seen the other cards; there was nothing on the back.

But on hers, a firm hand had written in black ink, "Pray for me." That was all.

CHAPTER 3

Eleanor and Bernice had marshaled their forces by the next day. By gentle persuasions, tears, and impassioned appeals, they attempted to change their father's mind. He would not be moved.

"I have promised," he said, his long nose haughty, the nostrils looking pinched. "And you should not speak as though this would be a poor match. He comes from a fine old family, finer than ours in England. He is related to the nobility, and is a man of honor and integrity."

Bernice wept again, and Eleanor looked grave and anxious. Viola retired to her duties, finding comfort in the garden. She was also appalled, but for a different reason. All that her father said confirmed that he had caused the tragedy five years ago. Her own beloved father, so fine and noble, in whom she had trusted all her life. Her heart wept, though her eyes were dry.

She would pause long over a delicate budding rose, touch the lilacs gently, sigh over the daffodils. She seemed to herself to have aged in but a few days. Death had never brushed so close to her, not since her own mother had died when Viola was so young she scarcely knew what was happening.

She had learned that Giorgio Michieli was twenty-eight years old. He seemed ageless in wisdom and cynicism. She had heard once that when one had actually faced the prospect of death, one was never young again. It was true, she thought. All the youth, and with it the joy and gladness, seemed dashed from him.

What had he been like as a youth? From her father's few words, she guessed at a picture: a handsome Italian of fervor and honor, eagerly volunteering for dangerous missions. Of a noble family, devoted to them and to his friends and country. With a profile like those on Roman coins—now marked heavily with that cruel scar.

She went each day to the small shrine in the villa they had rented. It was a room toward the back of the home, set apart, ignored by Viola's father and sisters. A fresco of Florence, from about the sixteenth century, covered one wall. Across another was draped a curtain of deep, gentle blue, and on it was hung a painting of the Madonna and Child by some seventeenth-century Italian artist, now unknown. Before it was set an ancient prayer stool, and Viola went daily to this and knelt on it, to pray earnestly.

Sometimes as she gazed at the face of the Madonna, she thought the Virgin smiled at her. A mere illusion of the sunlight that glinted across the painting, she reminded herself.

"If only I might help him," Viola said earnestly to the painted face. "Oh—I am young, I know. But he seemed kind and gentle to me. And he did ask me to pray for him. Oh, Madonna, they say you answer prayers, and intercede for us with Jesus. I beg you, help him if I cannot. Give him peace of soul, heal the scars in him, that he may find joy in life once more."

She would rise, somehow stronger and more confident. Yet when Giorgio Michieli came to their villa and sat quietly in their drawing room, she was ill at ease with him, and could find little to say. She listened eagerly when he spoke, and was glad when her father asked about the old days, or about Florence.

One afternoon, Sir Anthony asked about another matter, which seemed to bring a thundercloud to *Signor* Michieli's face. "I have wondered—what happened to the Doria family, your age-old enemies?"

Giorgio started, then set down his teacup, frowning. "You speak of them?" he said, his voice rather harsh.

"They were involved in all—all that matter," said Sir Anthony.

"Yes. Well—they retreated to their wolf-lair in the mountains near Pisa. I have not seen them since. I think they would not dare come to Florence again."

"Is it a sort of feud, what you call a vendetta?" Viola interposed timidly, too eager to restrain herself.

He looked at her, the dark eyes black with emotion. "Yes, *ma donna*, it is. Many years ago, they killed one of my ancestors, and of course the murder was avenged. They in turn have succeeded in killing much of my family—they were involved in the late wars, and took advantage of the violent times to murder. Why did you think of them, Sir Anthony?"

"Oh—" Sir Anthony shook his head, a little puzzled. "I thought I saw the old one, Enrico Doria, on the street the other day, when I was out near Fiesole. I must have been mistaken. I have not seen him for years, of course. Must have been someone who resembled the family."

"I hate all this talk of killing," said Bernice, with a little shudder. She was curled in her corner of the sofa, her pretty limbs drawn up a bit, her dark blond hair set off by a cream muslin gown. "Do let us speak of the ball tomorrow night instead!"

Her father smiled at her in affectionate amusement. "Yes, kitten, let us! Have you asked *Signor* Michieli if he will come with us?"

"Oh, you must come, *signore*," urged Eleanor. She had great charm, and her manners, no matter what she thought of the man, were impeccable. "I am sure you have an invitation, I urged it myself. You will come with us?"

Giorgio looked at her thoughtfully but said, "No, I thank you. You are most kind, but I do not care to mingle with crowds. I think people are more comfortable if I do not show my face, and remind them of what they wish to forget."

"Oh, but that is wrong," Viola burst out, from her seat behind the tea tray. "I am sure they would become accustomed to that, and surely you have earned your scars by your honorable actions! You should be proud of them, not wish to hide them!"

"Viola!" Eleanor rebuked her, flushing. She gave him an apologetic look. "She is very young, please pardon her."

"She speaks from a kind heart, and needs no pardoning. Indeed, I appreciate all you say, but I do not wish to attend such gatherings as yet. The injury to my leg gives me a problem at times. The fair ladies would not thank me for my awkward dancing."

So he put them off, but found reasons not to attend dinners either, no matter how small. Viola felt some regret for herself. Perhaps if *Signor* Michieli attended balls, she too might be allowed to attend.

The following evening, she felt all the more impatient with her youthfulness. Her sisters were busy at their dressing tables for hours, and she and her father sat alone in the drawing room. He needed no more than half an hour to get ready, and wished to relax before the long event.

"Father, will I be allowed to attend balls when I am eighteen?" she asked wistfully.

"I am sure your sisters will arrange everything to do with your coming out," he answered, without raising his head from the thin pages of the gazette he held.

She sighed and went to the piano, and began to play softly. She would entertain herself for a time; then after they left, she would have her dinner on a tray, and think of the gay time and the beautiful dresses which could be enjoyed at the ball. Some day she would go.

She began to sing a little Italian song that Carmela was teaching her: "Oh, love, you have my heart, and I have yours. What bliss we know, and shall it last forever? No one can part us, and eternity shall know of our devotion–"

Her father laid down the paper to listen to her, his eyes soft and distant. She knew he was thinking of her mother, Helen, who had died ten years ago. Since then he had turned colder and had become more and more devoted to his work.

When the song ended on a soft sigh, he said, "That is very pretty, my dear. How much like your mother you are!"

"She sings the Italian with much feeling," said a voice from the doorway. Both of them started, and turned about. *Signor* Michieli came in, the butler looking apologetic behind him.

"I would have announced him–" the servant began, but Giorgio waved him away.

"I stay but for one minute," he said. "I brought the papers of which I spoke, Sir Anthony."

Viola stood up uncertainly. "Shall I leave?" she murmured.

"No, no, it is but a minute–see, these are the ones."

Sir Anthony waved him to a chair and sat down again. He began to flick through the papers with interest. "Yes, yes, I had forgotten. Of course, that is correct–you are most accurate. Bonaparte had such a tight hold, the blockade–" He muttered over the papers, and Giorgio gave Viola a serious, intent look.

"You will play once more, *ma donna*?" he asked, as she sat uneasily on the small piano stool. "You have a lovely touch. Do you know other Italian songs?"

"I am just learning some."

"I beg you to sing again."

She gave him a shy smile, and turned to the piano again. She felt self-conscious singing a love song, but they were all that Carmela had taught her. She sang another in her sweet, true voice.

Hector McIntyre came in as Viola finished. "Very pretty, my dear, how beautifully you sing," he said gallantly, then saw the other man there.

Sir Anthony introduced them. The red-haired aide looked uncertainly at the stranger, bowed politely, and sat down. He was to make up one of their party.

Signor Michieli studied him frankly, with narrowed eyes. Hector did not seem to know what to make of the man, and conversation was stiff.

"But you are leaving shortly, I must make my departure," Giorgio said, and stood up. As he rose, the butler came in, and announced Reginald Selby and Niccolo Leopardo.

Viola had been gazing at Giorgio from her corner. She noted the jerk he gave, the strained way he stared at the doorway as the two men came in. Then an impassive mask seemed to descend over his features.

Not so the two men who entered. They stared incredulously, and Reginald Selby put up his hand as though in defense. "You—you are—" he began. "But this is impossible! You were dead—"

"The devil takes care of his own," Niccolo Leopardo said in Italian, but Viola understood him. Then he seemed to regain control of himself. "But what are you doing here? Do you still live in Florence?"

Sir Anthony interposed, with his usual sleek manner, but there was some hardness beneath it. "He is a guest in my home. You will not be insulting, no matter how you quarreled in the past over our methods," he said. Viola had never admired her father so much as when he stood there between them. "I believe you once fought together for our cause, however. Let that be remembered, and the rest forgotten."

"Florentines have long memories," said Giorgio Michieli, and with a polite bow he took his leave.

Selby did not wait until the door had closed before he voiced his fury. "Damn the villain! He dares to come here! How could you receive him, Sir Anthony? Have you forgotten how he deliberately wrecked our plans, the night of—"

Sir Anthony cut him off sharply. "He was not at fault. It is he who was betrayed. He was always loyal—"

"You are mad to think it," said Leopardo heavily. "I beg your pardon for my frank speaking, but you do not know the man. He is a most undesirable person. He comes from a tricky family, one that few persons can trust."

Viola was gazing from one to the other of them in surprise. Her father's face was flushed, his blue eyes glittering with fury. What was the cause of this difference in their attitude to Michieli? She noticed that Hector McIntyre, who had not spoken, was poised like a bristling dog in the presence of some danger he did not yet comprehend.

She had followed the Italian, most of it, and of course, all the English, as they had spoken quickly to each other. Now they seemed to calm themselves. Selby gave Leopardo a warning look as the older man seemed inclined to pursue the matter.

"But it is all over and done with," said Selby. "We must forget it. Nevertheless, Sir Anthony, I cannot warn you too strongly to have nothing to do with the man. The devil rose from the dead! God, I could not believe my eyes. Did you know nothing of this, *Signor* Leopardo?"

Niccolo Leopardo shook his head. "No, I have lived much in Pisa," he said. "And he must have kept to himself."

"I'll go hurry up the girls, we should be leaving," said Sir Anthony, and left the room abruptly. Viola wondered that he had not sent her instead, or summoned a maid. Then she realized he was going to warn the girls to say nothing of what Michieli wanted from their family.

But why the secrecy? Selby had been his most trusted aide in the late wars, and Leopardo had worked with them both. Why did he not want them to know of Giorgio Michieli's demands on him? She felt as perplexed as Hector McIntyre, scowling red-faced at the two other men.

Viola remembered her duties, and begged them all to be seated. Then she and Hector searched for some pleasant topic of conversation to entertain them for quite half an hour until her father returned, a daughter on each arm. The interval had been a strain, for the men had obviously remained upset and angry. The presence of the two girls immediately changed the atmosphere. All the men jumped up as they entered, beautiful and laughing. Eleanor was wearing a stunning ball gown of crimson, trimmed with golden feathers, and there were rubies in her ears. Bernice was equally resplendent in a ball gown of pale blue, finished with flounces from her waist to the tips of her blue slippers, and blue sapphires sparkled in her ears. The men gazed from one to the other.

"Juno and Venus," began Reginald Selby. "Or should I liken you to any goddess? They would pale in comparison—"

Bernice fluttered her blue feather fan at him, dimpling in pleasure. Eleanor condescended to give him a warm smile, while holding out her hand for Leopardo to kiss. He lingered over it, clasping her fingers warmly, greedily eyeing her.

Hector looked belligerent. Viola thought that the next day he would treat Eleanor to a diatribe on Italians and their hand-kissing ways, and how a lady should know better than to be taken in by foreigners. Amused, she knew just what he was thinking as he marched behind them out to the carriages.

No one seemed to have a thought for her. She sighed as they departed, and peeped from behind the crimson drapes to watch as they drove away.

She returned to the piano, for now her thoughts

drifted from the gay partygoers to the solitary man with the scarred face who had wished her to sing for him. Did he think of her, or had he come hoping for a glance from Bernice or Eleanor? Which did he favor? Whom did he come to see now?

And what was behind the different attitudes toward the man, the way Selby and Leopardo had treated him? They had been indignant, even horrified that he was still alive, furious that he was received. "Undesirable," Leopardo had said. In what way? His morals? Or because he had lost his money?

Viola frowned over her music, her thoughts drifting along idly with the notes. She sighed. There were so many mysteries, so many secrets in the world. She wondered if she would ever be allowed to know any of them. Or would they keep her a child forever?

Someday she would go to a ball, on the arm of a man who adored her. Her gray eyes filmed with dreams, as her fingers idly played on. She would be wearing a lilac dress of lace and silk, fragile as cobwebs. The skirt would be embroidered with pearls. She would wear amethysts about her throat, and an immense ring on her slim finger.

And the man who adored her would look at her and say, "You are more beautiful than a goddess. You are lovely as the dawn, you are my love—"

Her voice murmured the words of the song, "Oh, love, you have my heart—"

Her fingers paused on the keys. Something heavy and painful settled in her throat, she did not know why. She longed for something she could not identify. Love? Someone on whom to pour out the love and devotion which seemed bottled up inside her? Would any man ever want this? Or was she the one who would remain quietly at home, forever making her father comfortable, seeing her sisters off to balls, perhaps later taking care of their babies while they had a beautiful gay time. . . .

She was glad when the butler came in. "Your dinner is ready, Miss Viola. Shall I bring it here?"

"Oh—yes, please. I am—quite hungry." She jumped up to clear a space on a table.

He smiled down at her in fatherly fashion. "One day you shall go to the balls too, little *signorina*," he said, nodding his gray head. "When you are older—"

She flushed, that he had guessed how lonely and deserted she felt. "Yes, one day, when I am older," she said, with mock brightness.

She ate absently, aware of her loneliness, and thinking wistfully of the man who was also alone somewhere in this lovely city. Where did he go? Did he have a little room somewhere? With whom did he stay, or did he also sit over a table by himself?

CHAPTER 4

Viola's sisters slept late the next morning. Rising, she discovered that they had not returned until two in the morning. She felt very rebellious as she had breakfast alone in the vast dining room.

It was dark outside, the storm clouds had gathered, and the wind was cool. It would probably rain before the morning was over. But Viola felt very restless and impatient to remain in the house.

She called Carmela. "I shall go out in the carriage, Carmela. I cannot endure to remain indoors all the time."

Carmela gave her a wise look, and nodded. "Indeed, *Signorina* Viola. And perhaps we will go to some café. Why should you not enjoy yourself?"

It was comforting to find an ally. Viola gave her a radiant smile, and ran to find the rose cloak which would match her soft pink muslin dress. Because it might rain, she put on some half-boots that covered her ankles, and snatched up a deep bonnet of white with pink ribbons. Carmela was ready when her mistress was, stiff as a poker in her black, her thin face enlivened with curiosity and pleasure.

Bernardo was ready with the small carriage, his face beaming at them. "So you will go out, eh? Where shall you visit this day, little one?"

"Where shall we go?" asked Viola, hesitating. "What have I not seen yet?"

Carmela exchanged looks with Bernardo. "There is the Church of Santa Croce," Carmela suggested finally. "You will see the tomb of Michelangelo, the beautiful frescoes of our Giotto—"

Viola agreed at once, delighted, and they set out. Carmela was a great comfort to her. The middle-aged spinster told her eagerly about the church they would see, drifted to the life of Saint Francis, which was the subject of the frescoes, offered comments on the buildings and palaces along their way, and gossiped about some of the great families of Tuscany who lived there.

Viola finally asked the question that had hovered on the tip of her tongue. "Carmela, do you know the family of *Signor* Michieli, who has come to our home?"

The maid hesitated, her dark eyes narrowed a little. "But of course, *Signorina* Viola. All Florence knows of them, they are a noble family. All are dead, may God rest them in peace, but the good *signore* who comes."

"And they were noble and good?"

"Assuredly."

"And—and *Signor* Michieli—" Viola hesitated, flushing a little, but urged on by her troubled thoughts of the evening before. "He—is an honorable man?"

Carmela's eyes flashed. "All Florence knows of his courage, his honor, his integrity! Even when his own family endured the torture to which his scars testify, he did not break, he endured! He would have died before he revealed anything to his enemies!"

Bernardo was frankly listening, his ear turned to them. "What courage, what marvelous courage," he rumbled approvingly. "Of the best tradition, of something to make a song about. One is proud to know someone of his great courage!"

Viola, quite satisfied and happy, sank back in the carriage. Her father had said he believed in the man, and Viola did not care much for the opinions of Mr. Selby or *Signor* Leopardo. They continued through the narrow cobblestoned streets, between the great stone buildings, coming out into unexpected little squares with small cafés containing but a few tables and chairs. They passed a jewelry store, a small greengrocer, a butcher shop where hams hung in the doorway. She could not look enough, and twisted about with the frank curiosity of a child to see the busy shopkeepers in their blue aprons, the ladies in stiff black or smart colors, who shopped or paused to gossip.

Presently they came to the Church of Santa Croce. The white facade shone against the inlay of dark marble, outlined by the gray sky. Bernardo drove up to the very entrance, since it was beginning to rain, and Viola and Carmela slipped down and into the church.

They explored for more than an hour, fascinated by the timbered ceiling, the stained glass, the frescoes, the marble tombs of many famous citizens of Florence; all held Viola's interest. For a long time she studied the Bardi Chapel, with Giotto's frescoes, faded and delicately colored. Carmela explained in her brisk way that in the old days no one learned to read, not even some of the nobility. So these pictures had been painted to tell stories from the Bible and of the early Christian days. It would remind them of the sermons of their priests, and lift their thoughts to heaven.

Time slipped away, and finally they reluctantly left. Bernardo was watching for them, and drove up at once. "To home?" he suggested, peering up at Viola's face as he helped her into the carriage. "It comes to rain."

She felt rebellious again. Why should she dash home to see if her sisters had awakened from their long sleep after the dinner and ball? "No, I want coffee at one of those charming cafés," she said defiantly.

Bernardo grinned and shrugged. "As you will, *ma donna*," he said, and they set off.

Soon he reined the horses in and pointed. "There is a nice café here, *signorina*. You wish it?"

Since Bernardo recommended it, she nodded. She and Carmela were helped down, and rushed inside, for it had begun to rain once more. The owner bustled forward, bowing, immense in his great white apron.

"Come in, you are welcome," he said in Italian. Then he looked beyond her. Viola turned about as a deep voice spoke.

"Will you permit me to join you, *Signorina* Viola?" It was Giorgio Michieli, his eyes serious and intent.

Her heart gave a frightening leap; she felt as though she were choking. "Oh—oh, sir, of course," she managed to say. The owner was bowing and wiping off chairs in a great hurry, indicating the best table near the window for the *Signore*. Viola could not help noticing his abrupt change in manner, from politeness to awe; he showed an almost servile anxiety to please, as he showed *Signor* Michieli to a table.

Giorgio nodded, and held the chair for Viola. She sat down in a flutter of skirts. Carmela demurely accepted a chair at the next table, close enough to chaperone, far enough away to give them privacy.

Giorgio seated himself, and Viola gave him a shy look. He was again in dark clothes, today in dark blue. A sapphire sparkled in his white neckcloth. She was puzzled. If he lived in poverty, how could he dress so expensively? Had he saved some jewels?

"You will forgive me?" he was saying. "I recognized your carriage and the good Bernardo, and followed you. I hoped you would pause for refreshment."

"Oh—" She was stunned that he would wish to follow her and have coffee with her. She gave him a radiant smile. "Of course! How—how very pleasant." She rushed into further speech. "*Signorina* Pisani has been showing me the church of Santa Croce. It is indeed impressive and beautiful."

"You enjoy the art of my city," he said gravely. "I am extremely pleased. And you learn the Italian songs. Already you speak Italian very well."

"Carmela corrects my accent."

He gave the maid a nod and look of seeming approval. "She has the good Tuscan accent, the best in Italian language, so say we Florentines," he said, with some humor. She had never seen him smile, but today his look was softened, and the line of his mouth curved up a little.

Suddenly he saw something outside, through the rain which lashed against the great windows that lined two sides of the corner café. He said something to the café owner in swift Italian, and the man nodded quickly, and went to the door. He beckoned, and in came a flower seller with a wooden tray containing many blossoms.

The old woman in black came over to their table, blinked at the gentleman, and bowed as low as her wooden tray would allow. He looked at the great purple Parma violets, gathered them up in his scarred hands, and laid them before Viola. The woman stammered her gratitude as he placed some coins on the table, and waved her away.

"*Prego,*" he said, and turned to the café owner. "Give the woman coffee and cakes, as she wishes, until the rain is over." Then he looked at Viola. "You wish coffee, little one?" he asked her.

"Yes, please."

Steaming cups of coffee were brought swiftly, and plates of cakes. The old flower-seller was also served as quickly, by a young boy who gave Viola shy looks.

She unfastened the rose ribbons of her bonnet, and removed it with a sigh of relief. Then she unclasped her warm cloak, and Giorgio was quick to slip it from her. She felt his fingers brush her shoulders, and a little tremor of delight shook her. If only he did not think of her as a child!

"You wear rose today," he said. "It is a pleasure to see your brightness in the dull gray of our day."

"Thank you—*grazie*," she murmured, and saw him smile at last. The generous mouth curved upward, his brown eyes shone gently at her. He was attractive in spite of the scar on his tanned face.

"It is my pleasure. So you explore today. Tell me what you saw that you enjoyed especially."

He settled back, and his eyes sought her eager face again and again as they spoke. They drank coffee, rich with cream and sprinkled with chocolate flakes.

He had also chosen chocolate cakes, she observed, and noted his preference for the future.

Finally she dared to become more personal. "Please—will you tell me of your family, your ancestors in Florence?" she asked. "They—they played a large role in the history of the city, did they not?"

"Ah, yes," he said. "You wish to hear the old stories? Very well. You notice the square out here, which is the Piazza della Signoria. The name signifies that in the palace beyond the square, the officials of the government of Florence met to discuss problems. It was also the scene of a great joust. There was a siege of Florence, and the Florentines would not give in. Instead, they played games and laughed loudly, so that the enemies became furious and finally went away. Perhaps you know that Saint John the Baptist is our patron saint. He has the feast day of June twenty-fourth. On the twenty-fourth, we commemorate the day when the games were played, and Saint John saved the city by sending away the Germans who besieged us."

"Germans?" she asked, rather startled. "When was this?"

"In 1530. Yes, several centuries ago. Always we must fight those invaders who find our city attractive, and would plunder it."

Finding her intrigued, he went on to tell other stories, making the old cobblestoned square outside alive with costumed figures of the fifteenth and sixteenth centuries. He motioned toward the gaunt, crenellated palace opposite them, and told her how the great Medici family had their offices there, and how a passageway had been constructed across the second floor of the Uffizi Gallery to the river, across the old bridge called the Ponte Vecchio, to the Pitti Palace, so that one might go the complete way without ever stepping outside.

"There were always enemies waiting to kill," he said. "When one is wealthy and powerful, one always has enemies. However, if the people respect one, and will come to one's aid, one will keep the power, for the power rests eventually in the people. One should have respect for all, and treat them with honor and integrity. Then one will earn the right to call on the people for aid in time of danger."

She gazed up at him thoughtfully, so fascinated she would forget to drink her coffee. He told her of the later Medici, of how they married Spanish royalty, who had brought intrigue and poison to the politics of Florence. "Ah, how the people missed the goodness of the great Lorenzo, and of his grandfather, the wily Cosimo. Now it was all who shall kill whom, and the good days were over for a long time," he said. "Many fine men were exiled from their beloved Florence. Dante wrote in exile, you know. You have read his poetry?"

"Only in English," she said regretfully, secretly resolving to have Carmela teach her the Italian of Dante.

Sometimes when he spoke of the battles and the intrigues, his face hardened, and his eyes flashed sparks. He was a tough, hard man, who had fought for himself and his city. He almost growled the words, as he spoke of the late wars, and how the French and Austrians had tried to divide Florence between them.

"But enough of battles," he said suddenly, with another of his strangely attractive smiles. "I shall tell you of the tournaments of love. You see, the great Lorenzo de' Medici was a famous lover as well as a politician. He enjoyed seeing the beauty of lovely women. So on special days, carriages would go by, full of beautiful ladies, the most glorious of Florence, all dressed in their jewels and silks, and some scarcely dressed at all—ah, do I shock you?"

"A little," she admitted, flushing. "Carmela did tell me of the ladies who wore so little, and nothing much over their—" Her small hand indicated her slight bosom. "Just flowers, I think."

"Flowers and jewels," he said. "Then the Queen of Beauty would be crowned amidst all her attendants, and there would be a mock-joust in the piazza outside here. When you see the paintings of Sandro Botticelli, you will observe the beautiful ladies he adored to paint, one of them rumored to be the favorite of Lorenzo de' Medici, one Simonetta Vespucci. Or perhaps she was the adored of his brother, the Giuliano de' Medici, slain by the Pazzi family in their conspiracy."

"Oh, tell me of that!" she demanded. "Carmela told me a little in the cathedral, where it happened."

So he told her the story of how Lorenzo and his brother, the handsome Giuliano, had come to the cathedral to worship, and had been attacked by prearrangement by the rival Pazzi family. Giuliano had been slain. Lorenzo had escaped to one of the chapels, while his attackers were slain in turn.

"If they had murdered the great Lorenzo, the entire history of our country might have been different," he said thoughtfully. "Praise God, he was spared, and went on to become one of our greatest rulers of Florence, wise and just and good. He was the patron of Michelangelo, and encouraged many sculptors and artists and writers."

Seeing her face so distressed over the account of the slayings, he quickly changed the subject again.

"Would you like to have been one of the queens of beauty, *Ma donna* Viola? Indeed, your loveliness, your blond hair, and great gray eyes would have been sure to attract the attention of the de' Medici," he said in teasing tones. "However, would you have been willing to wear so little?"

She did flush then. He had never before spoken to her in such a personal way. "Oh—I don't know. Times change, do they not?" she said in a confused way, her hand fluttering to her coffee cup. "Eleanor did tell me that in London t—there is a fashion—the ladies dampen their muslin dresses until they cling, and are very revealing. But only the most daring of ladies will wear the fashion."

"And I am sure your father would not permit any of his lovely daughters to do so," he said, more gently. "He is very protective of all of you."

"Yes, of course," she said, but she could not help thinking her father cared most for Eleanor. Still, he was watchful over them all, as Giorgio said.

Carmela had been making anxious movements for the past ten minutes, and Bernardo kept poking his dark head in the doorway of the café. The rain had let up. "I—I fear I must depart," Viola said, with a reluctant sigh. "It grows late."

He drew out a gold watch on a long gold chain and consulted it gravely. "Ten minutes past one o'clock," he said. "Is that late, *Ma donna* Viola?"

She stared at him, her hands at her lips. "Oh—oh, dear! It is—we lunch at one, and my sisters—oh, dear, I must fly—"

She jumped up. He rose reluctantly, and assisted her into her cloak. "The rain has paused," he said, "and the sun has come out. I had thought it was the radiance of your smile that had lightened the sky."

She blinked up at him, then gave him a shy smile. "Oh, you are teasing me. Will you—come to luncheon?" she asked.

He hesitated, then shook his head. "I will follow you, however, in my carriage, and make sure you arrive safely home, little one," he said. And she had to be satisfied with that.

He did follow then, in a smart black phaeton drawn by two black horses. She was puzzled again. If he had lost all, how was he able to keep such a carriage? Or did he borrow it from a friend? Probably, she decided.

At her home, he bowed, lifted his tall hat, and went on his way without coming in. She raced inside, to be greeted with reproaches when she finally came to the dining table, flushed and breathless from hurrying.

"Where have you been?" Sir Anthony said sternly. "I knew only that you had departed early in your carriage. Only the fact that *Signorina* Pisani and Bernardo were with you prevented me from going out to find you."

"Oh, Father, I am so sorry." She gave him a quick kiss on his cheek, and hurried to her place. She looked guiltily at her sisters and at Hector McIntyre. "Please forgive my rudeness. I was—learning much more of the history of Florence, and the time sped away. Then it rained, and I took shelter in a café, and—"

"You must not do this again," said Eleanor, quite crossly. "Do you realize we had to rush about and plan the luncheon, after a late night? And we must go out to tea almost at once, and nothing has been done about the dinner tonight? Do you expect us to do your work, while you moon about the city?"

Viola went limp, and stared down at her plate

shamefacedly. She could not confess before her father and Hector that she had been listening to a man who entranced her, that she had wanted to stay on and on. "I am sorry," she mumbled.

"Well, don't let it happen again," said Bernice. "I wanted you to do my hair, and now there is no time."

"You cannot neglect your duties like this," Eleanor went on, her mouth tight. Her tone was smooth and controlled, but with an edge of anger. "You came to Florence with us to help, not to race about like a giddy child."

Viola's face burned at being rebuked before Hector McIntyre, who was beginning to look quite sorry for her. She murmured her apologies yet again, and subsided, but she had no appetite for luncheon. The others finished and left her, her father, and Hector to return to work, her sisters to complete their toilettes and go out.

It had quite destroyed the pleasure of her morning. What would they say if they knew with whom she had spent those hours? Well, they didn't have to know, she thought rebelliously. They dashed about in fine clothing, enjoying many pleasures. Why should she not enjoy the company of the one man she admired above all others?

The butler bent over her. "You will have your veal, Miss Viola?" he murmured. "It is a very tender piece, the chef saved it for you."

To please him, and because his thoughtfulness cheered her, she ate it, and had a cup of coffee and some ice cream for dessert. Her mind was made up. She would continue to go about, more cautiously, of course, and learn the history of Florence, and see the beautiful paintings and sculpture that Giorgio Michieli had told her about. Even if her sisters did not care about that, she did, and she could continue to do so.

Before plunging into her work for the evening's dinner party, Viola slipped back to her bedroom and arranged her violets, which Carmela had put in water. Then she paused briefly, her face pressed into the flowers, drawing on their subtle scent.

One day, someone might love her, and rescue her from all this. One day, someone might give her flowers in love, and press her hand, and kiss her lips. One day, her sisters might not have the power to order her about, and leave her to work while they hurried to their entertainments, and gossiped with their friends.

Oh—one day, her wistful heart murmured, someone might want the love and devotion she longed to pour out. And he would bring her flowers and sweets, and smile at her, and his eyes would light up to see her coming, and he would be fine and honorable. . . .

Like Giorgio, she thought. Someone like Giorgio Michieli, brave and good, and dependable. He would not look at her in that way, he thought her a child. But when she was grown up—one day, one day.

CHAPTER 5

Another week slipped past. It was close to the end of April. Viola continued to go out in the mornings, but was cautious to return by twelve, so that her sisters would not complain to her father, and perhaps stop these precious expeditions.

Giorgio Michieli came to the villa several afternoons. Once Viola baked some special chocolate cakes for him, and saw him look at her as he took one on his plate. She nodded a little, and thought he almost smiled. He smiled so little—he was not happy, she thought. He always seemed troubled and distant.

Then one day he came early, and went to her father's study. Viola heard the voices going on and on, her father's voice, and Giorgio's, deeper and more deliberate. Bernice came to the drawing room, looking pale. "Is it—him?" she asked, in some distaste. "I wonder if he has made up his mind? Surely Father will not force me to marry him!"

Viola looked down at her embroidery, a little blindly. "Eleanor is the eldest," she said colorlessly. "She has much presence and charm."

Bernice shuddered delicately, her slim shoulders moving in the cream dress. She crossed to the fireplace and held out her beautiful hands to the flames. Eleanor came softly into the room, rather subdued in a dark blue dress with velvet trimmings about the long sleeves and hem.

"He is here again?" she murmured. "Viola, you have ordered tea?"

"Yes, Eleanor." They were all tense, feeling his decision must be near. Perhaps, thought Viola, pausing in her sewing, he might have changed his mind. He seemed softened; his thoughts might have turned from revenge to forgiveness. He appeared to enjoy his conversations with her father; she thought they respected each other.

Presently the two men came in from the study. Sir Anthony seemed pale, but relaxed. Giorgio Michieli was stern as he bowed to the three girls and greeted them.

After the first formalities, Sir Anthony said, "*Signor* Michieli has something to say to you." And to emphasize the seriousness of the moment, he stood up and went to the mantel where Bernice had stood, and clasped his hands behind his back.

Viola set down her embroidery carefully. Her hands shook, and she folded them in her lap. She could not look at him, or at her sisters. She felt almost dizzy with apprehension.

Giorgio Michieli looked deliberately at each girl in turn, Viola last, his eyes half screened by the long lashes. "Yes. As you recall, I have said to your father that I wish one of you in marriage. He will settle a dowry of one hundred thousand pounds on that girl, and we shall be married within the week. Upon careful consideration, I have decided to request the hand of *Signorina* Viola in marriage."

The girls were struck dumb. All gazed up at him with wide eyes, Eleanor shocked and white, Bernice blinking with relief, Viola in sheer amazement. Her heart was throbbing wildly; she could scarcely hear for the blood drumming in her ears. Had she heard correctly?

Giorgio went to her and held out his hand. She took it, her own hand cold and shaking, and let him draw her up.

"You will agree to this, little one?" he asked quietly.

"Oh–yes, if you wish it," she said simply. He seemed to draw a deep breath of–what was it, relief? she wondered. Yet she scarcely noticed his reaction, for she saw her sisters' bodies almost sag with the release of tension, and noted the little wink of satisfaction that her father gave Eleanor. They were relieved that Eleanor had not been chosen, or Bernice.

She scarcely knew what was happening. All she knew was that she would do anything–she had promised the Blessed Virgin she would do anything!–to make up for what her father had done to this gentleman. And she would be helping her sisters, for they did not wish to marry him, they shrank from him.

And Giorgio–she liked and respected him, and trusted his integrity. He would never hurt her, she thought. So when his fingers closed warmly over hers, she let her small fingers clutch at his in answer. He bent and lifted her hand to his lips, and gently kissed the tips of her fingers.

"But she is very young," Eleanor said finally, anxiety in her tone. Viola remembered how good her eldest sister had been all these years, how she had tried to take the place of her mother, and direct and advise her. "She has not been presented at court—or anything!"

"She may now attend balls," said Giorgio, with cool amusement in his tone. "As a married lady, I am sure you will not object if I escort her!"

"Of—of course," said Eleanor blankly, and came over to kiss Viola's cheek and shake Giorgio's hand. Bernice recovered sufficiently from her astonishment to do the same, her dimples flashing teasingly as she gazed up at him.

Then he took out a leather case from his pocket, and opened it. He reached for Viola's left hand, and placed on it a large ring. Viola stared at it, stunned. It was a huge, dark blue sapphire, with fire in its depths, and set about with sparkling diamonds.

About her small wrist he placed a matching bracelet of square-cut sapphires alternating with tiny diamonds. "These are family pieces. I hope they will please you," he said, and gave her a gentle look. "It was necessary to have the ring cut down a little, your hand is such a tiny one."

"Oh, they are very beautiful, thank you," she whispered. Her wrist felt heavy, her hand unnatural, with the immense ring on it. The girls came close to admire it, staring in surprise at the precious gems.

"So—it is arranged," said Giorgio, with calm satisfaction. He pushed Viola gently to her seat on the sofa, then seated himself beside her. "About the wedding, *carina*, will you be ready in one week? My family church is that of San Marco. I think you have not yet seen it. I shall accompany you there. The priest is anxious to meet you, and all will be arranged."

She swallowed. He was watching her closely. She

kept her face serene only by an intense effort. A week—and she would be a married woman! Subject to his will—that of a stranger—belonging to him, living in his home—"I shall be ready, *signore*," she whispered. "What—what shall I wear?"

"It is not usual, but I should like to help choose your wedding dress. A dressmaker of my acquaintance will make it. May I take you there this afternoon? She will measure you, and show you various patterns, and the veil."

Eleanor spoke up, seeming to overcome her amazement and beginning to reassert herself. "I shall come with you, of course. Viola has not often chosen her own clothes. There are styles which suit her—"

"Thank you, you are most kind," said Giorgio. But when they went to the dressmaker a little later, it was neither Eleanor nor Viola who chose the gown, it was Giorgio. He had, it seemed, very definite ideas of what he wished.

He chose the pattern of a very simple dress, with a square neck set about with Italian lace. The bodice was tight to the curved waist, the skirt full to the ankles and swept into a little train of lace. The sleeves were puffed above the elbows, then tight to the wrist, ending in lace cuffs. Over it she would wear a sheer lace veil which Giorgio chose from among those the dressmaker showed him.

The dressmaker's manner was strange to the girls. She almost curtsied to the floor in awe. Everything was "Immediately, *signore*. At once, sir. It shall all be done quickly, as you direct, *signore*. Of course, all other work shall stop, we shall work only on what you wish—"

Giorgio seemed unaffected by her manner. But Eleanor whispered later to Viola that the woman must have known his family at one time. "Wasn't it peculiar that she should bow down to him? Of course, he may not be as poor as we thought—those jewels, my dear! Let me see them again!"

Now that her sisters had recovered from their relief, they were inclined to be a little jealous of the jewelry, the wedding gown, the attentions. Flowers arrived daily from Giorgio. He would come in two days to take her in the morning to the church of San Marco, to meet the priest and arrange the wedding, which would be held in one of the small chapels there, since Viola was not Catholic. She asked Giorgio timidly if he wished her to become a Catholic.

"This is a decision you may make in time, *carina*," he said. "I have told the priest you are not to be pressured into this. Later you may take instruction, and if you wish to be baptized in the faith, it will be so."

"But what do you wish?" she asked, puzzled.

He patted her hand, as though she were a child. "For you to be happy and carefree," he said vaguely. "Now, your sisters and your papa will join us at the church—about twelve, shall we say? After we speak to the priest I wish to show them the villa where we shall live, my family home for many centuries. It is a little way up into the hills."

Eleanor looked puzzled at the invitation. "You wish us to see your home? Do you wish us to purchase some furniture and linens for Viola?"

He looked at her, his mouth curved rather cynically. "That will not be necessary, though you must do as you please," he said politely.

Eleanor said that night to Viola, as she talked to her in the drawing room, "That might solve the problem of what to give you as a wedding gift. Papa is giving you all that money, but you may need it to live on, and pay the servants—if you have servants. Oh, dear. Poor little Viola. It is a good thing you do know how to cook!"

Viola had another thought, more pressing. She wished to take Carmela with her, but she did not know if Giorgio could afford her maid's salary. Would he permit her to keep Carmela, and pay for her herself? She hardly knew how to ask. Carmela had no such doubts, it seemed, and was already packing her possessions to move with her mistress, talking gaily of what good times they would have.

Giorgio called for Viola in the morning, in a huge carriage that would have held six people, and driven by a coachman in purple and gold livery. Viola was more and more bewildered. Was some kind friend loaning him all this fine stuff? She longed to see his home, to know how she might plan. She did not care if it was a small cottage. She would make it as comfortable and as happy for him as she could.

The priest exhibited some of the same behavior as the dressmaker, surprising her all the more. Everything would be as *Signor* Michieli wished it. Flowers would be arranged, *si, si,* and there would be altar boys, and the service would be in Italian and English, as well as Latin.

They talked so rapidly in Italian that Viola could not follow them, and finally gave up trying. Then it was almost twelve, and Giorgio took her arm and pressed it gently. "Time to go, *carina.* Your father will be waiting, I believe."

He gazed down at her, a hint of mischief in his face.

"Ah, I wonder if you will like my house?" he murmured, and took her outdoors into the sunlight. Her sisters and her father were there, waiting in their carriage. Giorgio directed them to follow, and they set out.

It turned out to be a ride of more than an hour. Viola became more and more curious as they climbed up and up the hills toward Fiesole. Each view was more glorious, of Florence nestled in the valley, of the villas that peeped from behind trees along the way. Homes were set well back from the road and surrounded by stone walls, but they could glimpse gardens, and fountains, and twisted gray-green olive trees.

The carriage finally turned off into a wide driveway, lined with cypresses like pure black flames curling up into the sapphire sky. Beyond were well-trimmed hedges, an irregular fish pond of immense size, a fountain with a pert imp and a dolphin playing in the center while water splashed gently about them. Several beds of formal flowers were arranged about the green lawns—roses and columbine, peonies, delphiniums of azure blue and purple. Larkspur of scarlet, pink, blue, mauve and white—Viola could scarcely take it all in.

Then she saw the square-shaped villa, pale gold, and set amid the green lawns like a topaz. As they neared the end of the winding drive, she saw that the golden pillars lined the front from the ground to the top of the second floor. The wide doors were open, huge wooden doors studded with nails, and carved with some design. As she came closer, she saw it was his crest—immense sea dragons curling about in rough-cut waves.

"Your home—" she whispered. He was holding her hand, and felt her tremble. This was either a jest, or a disaster! He could not live here, not here in this mansion! This castle!

"My home, soon to be yours also," he said quietly. "I hope you will be very happy here, Viola. You are very young, but you have a sweetness of spirit and a determination of will, a curiosity of mind which I enjoy. We shall be great friends, shall we not?"

What a curious way to speak! He was supposedly bent on revenge, and had chosen her because of some odd whim. Yet now he spoke of making her happy—in a castle!

"It is so huge!" She turned to him in distress. "I thought you lived in a cottage, Giorgio!"

He flicked one finger at her flushed cheek, teasingly. "Disappointed? Then I shall build you a cottage on the grounds, that you may play in it!"

He was treating her like a child again. Oddly ashamed, she fell silent, even when they entered the mammoth doors and she heard her sisters gasp and murmur their astonishment. Only her father seemed grave and preoccupied as the butler in purple and gold livery took their cloaks and conducted them to the first drawing room.

They walked over marble floors in a checkerboard pattern of black and white, past huge mahogany tables set with mosaic patterns of birds and flowers. Immense vases of Florentine pottery stood on the tables, filled with tall spikes of gladioli, graceful branches of willow, and elegant roses. Giorgio conducted Viola into an immense drawing room, and finally she could not restrain an exclamation.

"Oh, how beautiful, how very beautiful!"

He seemed pleased with her enthusiasm. Her sisters were now speechless. Viola glanced at them and saw twin expressions of sheer envy and astonishment twisting their pretty features.

The walls of the formal drawing room were covered with patterned green silk brocade. The chandeliers were of Austrian crystal, delicately curved. Viola could imagine its brilliance when the candles had all been lit. The ceiling was carved and gilded with nymphs and cupids peering from the corners. About the room were scattered rosewood sofas and chairs, some covered in purple brocade, some in green velvet.

"Please be seated. Luncheon will be served in a few minutes." Giorgio, in his own setting, seemed to take on more dignity and nobility, Viola thought, settling herself uneasily on the edge of a purple brocaded chair, with wide, curved arms. She felt the arms soft beneath hers. The chair was so comfortable, yet so formally beautiful.

He spoke rapidly to a servant, and turned back to them.

"After luncheon I should like to show you some of the rooms. Also Viola must see the suite which will be hers. They have been redecorated, and I hope she will approve of the colors." He bowed formally to Viola, his face serious.

She was more bewildered than ever. Redecorated? For her? When had he planned all this? Had he chosen her from the beginning, not at the last minute, as she had thought?

He seemed to be watching her closely. She glanced up at him from behind her long lashes, her eyes troubled. He took her hand gently and squeezed it. "Later," he said, too quietly for anyone else to hear.

Her spirits rose. Perhaps he would tell her that he had come to love her, that he had decided to marry her because he admired and liked her very much. That it was not a marriage for revenge, as they had thought at first. She felt she did not understand, but surely all would soon come right.

The butler announced luncheon, and Giorgio led them in, with Viola on his arm. He placed her at his right hand at one end of the immense table; on its highly polished surface was set the splendid silver. The cream-colored china was bordered in purple and decorated with a small sea dragon crest in gold. She thought the delicate porcelain must be many years old.

She glanced toward the place indicated for her at the end of the table, opposite Giorgio at the head. He seemed to understand her thoughts. For her ears alone, he murmured, "There is a smaller dining room for when we dine alone. This is used only for formal occasions. One needs to shout very loudly to be heard from one end to the other, eh?"

She smiled, and felt more at ease with his humor. She became aware, as a footman served them, that they were being peeped at from the two doorways that led into the room. A maid would glance in, then duck out. An older woman, stiff in black, peered fixedly at her before departing. Giorgio became aware of them, and frowned at the footman, giving him orders in swift Italian.

He turned to her to apologize. "They are all curious to see their new mistress, Viola. I hope you will not be offended. I shall introduce you at some later time. I told them you are like an English porcelain doll, with blond hair and gray eyes, and an immense sweetness. They all wish to meet you."

"Oh, how charming," exclaimed Eleanor, smiling at Viola. "I think you will have no trouble at all with the servants, Viola. I am sure you will be pampered and spoiled, if Giorgio has his way."

He nodded at her approvingly. "Yes, that is what I mean to do, exactly," and they all laughed a little, and relaxed, even Sir Anthony.

The luncheon was delicious. The first course was of cold seafood—shrimp, chopped fish, mussels, and other things Viola did not recognize, all dressed in a light, creamy but spicy sauce. The next course was broiled chicken, chopped with red and green peppers, and served with zucchini. With it was served a crisp green salad. The final course was a selection of cheese arranged on a great wooden board, and a bowl of fruit. Giorgio picked out what he wished Viola to try, mentioning the names of some of the cheeses. And with each course was an appropriate wine, a white one with the fish, a stronger rosé with the chicken, red wine with the cheese.

"Excellent, excellent," said Sir Anthony, finally drawing back with a sigh of pleasure. "My compliments to the chef."

Giorgio spoke to the footman, who beamed. "The chef has been with our family since his boyhood. He will be most pleased."

"I would like to show you some of the rooms first, then we may have coffee in one of the drawing rooms," said Giorgio, rising when the ladies indicated they were finished. He held Viola's chair. "I am anxious to see whether you are pleased."

"I cannot help but be pleased, I am sure of it," she said impulsively. "You must have gone to great trouble."

"Not at all, not at all. It gave me great pleasure." He escorted her up the wide circular staircase to the next floor, and they walked along the parquet floors to a room at the end of the hallway. He flung wide the door and led her in.

She was speechless again. If he had consulted her carefully he could not have chosen better. The room was enormous, with full-length French windows that gave onto a balcony. The draperies, the Persian rug, the brocaded walls, even the furniture, were all in white or in shades of blue and violet. As Viola looked about the splendid room, her attention fixed on a delicate desk with a chair covered in pale blue velvet, set in one corner. Here she would do her accounts and writing, for the entrancing pigeonholes and drawers indicated the desk was as practical as it was lovely. On it had been set a porcelain bowl filled with lilies of the valley.

Involuntarily she looked about for a bed. The sofas were too narrow—no—and there were two coffee tables, and other small rosewood tables set about.

"This is your drawing room, Viola. I hope it pleases you. Here is your bedroom." And Giorgio strode across the precious Persian rug to another door. He opened it, and stood aside for her to enter another room, almost as large. In the center was a huge canopied bed, with four tall posts carved with dolphins and sea dragons rioting around the curves. The canopy was of rose brocade, matching the long draperies before the windows. Several comfortable-looking plush-covered chairs were set about. Her dressing table was of shining rosewood, with a mirror set low between two taller sections of drawers. Giorgio opened the wardrobe doors, showing the mirrors set inside, and also the immense space for her clothing.

Her sisters seemed to be recovering their voices. Bernice flung open one door and discovered a large bathroom fitted with a tub, a washstand of white porcelain, another mirrored door, and delicate porcelain appointments in cream with violets sprinkled in a delicate pattern. Eleanor tried another door but found it bolted. Giorgio looked at her.

"That leads to my rooms," he said. "They are not quite completed."

"Oh!" It was the self-possessed Eleanor who blushed now, and sent a quick look at her youngest sister. Giorgio looked at Viola.

"If anything displeases you, you have but to say—" he began.

"Oh—everything is so beautiful, I could not be more pleased," she murmured. "I cannot believe they are for me! It is too much. All these lovely rooms—"

"The house is yours," he said quietly, but seemed happy with her shining face. He led them back downstairs to a smaller drawing room to have their coffee, then escorted them back to their villa in Florence.

Viola was very silent that night. She had many confusing thoughts. Why had he not told them he was wealthy and respected? Why had he allowed them to think him poor and despised? Why, he could have any girl in Florence, or in all Europe, for that matter! Girls would leap at the chance to ally themselves with an old and revered family—when the owner was obviously wealthy! Why then—why—why?

Her sisters were livelier that night, unable to refrain from gushing on about the villa, and their brother-in-law to be. When Reginald Selby came for dinner, he must learn all! But Selby did not believe them at first.

The Englishman turned quite pale as Bernice cried out the news. "You do not mean it! I never dreamed the friendship had gone so far! You will allow Miss Viola to marry him? That villain, that traitor—"

Sir Anthony stopped him sternly. "He is my friend. I am proud our family will be allied with his."

"And he is a wealthy man, after all," Bernice added. "We saw his villa—it is full of expensive objects! Why, I saw jade statuettes set about on tables, and ivory in cabinets, and he has given Viola the most beautiful jewels—show him, Viola—" And she grabbed her sister's arm and held it out.

Reginald Selby was stammering in indignation. "But this cannot be! Whatever persuaded you to agree to such a match? I thought you agreed with me that he was a criminal, a fellow of the worst type—"

"Nonsense!" said Sir Anthony, becoming flushed with anger. "I never agreed with you about this. Nonsense. He is of a fine family, the last of his family—"

"He has done some dark deeds! I myself know of three chaps he murdered—"

Sir Anthony hushed him sternly, and led him to his study. The older girls looked questioningly after them, but Viola slipped away to her room, to ponder in private. Why, indeed, had Giorgio Michieli chosen to marry her? What lay beyond that dark, scarred face? He had no more need of her dowry than would a prince.

CHAPTER 6

Giorgio and Viola were married the first week of May. The dressmaker had come every day with her assistants, and the white wedding dress was set in the wardrobe, covered with a sheet, to await the day of the ceremony. The dressmaker continued to come, though, bearing fine silks to be made in other gowns for Viola—ruffled blue silks for day gowns, a violet ball gown of gauze and pearls, rose velvet day dresses, evening dresses, and all manner of bonnets and slippers and gloves to match.

The older girls could not restrain their admiration, mingled with frank envy. Sir Anthony had to promise them more dresses before they would be quiet. But he disclaimed any ability to match the jewels that arrived with each visit of Giorgio.

Viola's fiancé brought fine leather cases each day, and opened them quietly to display to Viola what he wished to give her. A beautiful strand of pearls to be worn with her wedding dress, and pearl earrings and bracelet. A stunning set of amethysts in a huge ring, bracelet, earrings, and necklace. A set of topaz. She felt overwhelmed, stunned by it all.

"There are others being remodeled for you. I hope you will be pleased," he said, seemingly anxious only to make her happy.

Yet—did he understand her so little that he thought she would be made happy with dresses and jewels? Did he think she longed to live in a villa fine as a castle? When he arrived, he would kiss her hand, and sit near her, and pay her attentions that were thoughtful and kind. He sometimes brought her chocolates, and flowers came daily with his card. But no message in his bold black handwriting was written on the card. No personal word made her feel she was loved. What did he wish of her?

It was subtle torture, she thought once, with a great sigh. Perhaps this was what he meant to do. He knew she was sensitive, that she adored her father and sisters and was anxious to please them. Did taking her away from them constitute his revenge on the family? But surely he could see that they were relieved at his choice. Eleanor had frankly confided it would make her shudder to have the kisses of such a scarred fellow, and Bernice had shivered at the very thought of belonging to him. They had heard more dark stories of him from Reginald Selby. Few in Florence had heard yet of the wedding, and Viola wondered if Giorgio meant to keep it secret until too late.

Yet—her father trusted him!

It was all too confusing for her to understand. She clung to the thought that she wished to comfort him in his sorrow over the loss of his family, and she resolved to be the best possible wife for him.

Her wedding day dawned bright and clear, without a sign of fog, or even a clinging white cloud. The sky shimmered like blue silk. Viola rose early, dressed in a wrapper, and went to the little chapel. She knelt before the Virgin and murmured her prayers over and over—that she might make Giorgio happy, and help him recover from the scars of his experiences.

For herself, she dared not even think.

Sir Anthony and the girls drove with her in the carriage to the Church of San Marco. Viola, behind the white veil, was suddenly aware that there was a large crowd in the square before the church, and that dozens of carriages lined the streets nearby.

"I wonder what is going on. A festival?" her father said, frowning slightly.

The faces of the crowd turned toward them, and their silence when they saw the bride was vaguely frightening to Viola. She had never been the center of attention before, and she felt as though everyone in the world was staring at her.

Her father escorted her on his arm into the church, her sisters following. More people were inside, in the pews and standing in the aisles near the small chapel. And suddenly, Viola realized all these people had come to see her married!

All these people, and she scarcely knew a one! But they looked toward Giorgio, and a murmur arose when he bowed to his bride as she approached the altar. It was a friendly murmur, of warmth and appreciation. Viola stepped forward to him, and took the hand he extended as though it might be a lifeline.

The service began. Viola knelt on the white satin cushion before her, and solemnly exchanged vows with Giorgio. She had trembled before; now she was quiet and calm. She saw the kind, elderly face of the priest, heard him speaking clearly in Latin, then a little sermon in English and in Italian. All was silent behind them, except for an occasional rustling in the great crowd.

It was over so quickly. She had said the words, and listened to the prayers, and heard the bells rung, and smelled the incense as it swung about them. Giorgio put his hand under her elbow and helped her rise. She was intensely aware of the simple gold ring he had placed on her finger next to the great sapphire.

She turned about, and received her father's kiss on her cheek. While he was shaking Giorgio's hand, her sisters kissed her, and gave her warm wishes for her happiness.

She glanced timidly toward the great crowd, and saw the British minister, an associate of her father, approach her smilingly. She had not been aware of his presence. His wife was introduced, and then several others came up to speak to the bride.

But Giorgio was frowning, and shaking his head, and finally the crowd fell away, and allowed them to depart. He said tightly to Viola, "I do not know how word got about. I am very sorry for this."

"It is quite all right," Viola assured him, intensely puzzled. It was as though the crowd disturbed him greatly, and his dark eyes constantly searched the gathering. She was aware of anger surging up in him.

"No, it is not," he said curtly, and escorted her to his carriage. The crowd saw them and raised a cheer. Reluctantly he paused and lifted his hand, clasping Viola's, over their heads. Then he said something rapidly in Italian. She thought it was something about "comrades," but she was not certain.

At last he followed her into the carriage, and his grooms shouted for the crowd to give way, which they did, with much good-natured jostling.

They drove to a nearby restaurant, where her father had ordered a dinner. But Giorgio seemed uneasy and preoccupied, unlike himself. The meal was soon over, and they departed. The waiters had hovered over them in a private room, but people had peeped in the doors and windows to see them.

Finally they were on their way up to the villa. Viola was musing about the wedding, the strange way the crowd had gathered, Giorgio's puzzling reaction. She wanted to ask him about it, but his scowl of suppressed anger halted her. She decided on silence. It was usually the best path when her father was angry.

Carmela had been at the wedding, and followed them home in another carriage with several footmen and the butler, who had also attended. When they arrived at the villa, she hurried to Viola in her new grand suite, as the girl stood uncertainly in the middle of the bedroom.

"Oh, Miss Viola—pardon me, *Signora* Michieli!" she cried merrily. "Did you ever see such a crowd? How they honored him—and you. I was so proud."

"Why did they come?" asked Viola impulsively. "I could not ask—him. Why did they all come?"

"Why?" Carmela seemed shocked. "But they—they are friends and admirers of the *Signore*! All Florence had word of his wedding day! Did one think no one would show respect this day?" And she went bustling about, happily scolding to herself in Italian, helping Viola change to a simple violet muslin dress. She had left the girl more puzzled than ever.

Carmela persuaded Viola to rest, which she was glad enough to do. She reclined on a violet lounge in her fine drawing room, overlooking the immaculate green lawns and clipped hedges of the gardens. She had much to occupy her mind. Giorgio had been pleased with his friends, yet—yet angry, worried. He had searched the crowd, studied the faces, glanced sharply at the rooftops. What had he feared or expected? That was the puzzle.

Carmela came after two hours, and said that the *Signore* was waiting for her in the smaller drawing room, and she would accompany her there. The maid seemed to have become quickly acquainted with the huge villa, and confidently led her mistress down the winding stairs to the huge hallway, and off to the left to the blue and cream drawing room she remembered from the first visit.

Giorgio was standing at the windows, his hands behind his back. He had changed to less formal attire, she noticed. When he turned to meet her as she came in, she almost exclaimed aloud at the lines of strain on his face and the gravity of his expression. But he took her hand gently. "And how are you? Quite rested, Viola?"

"Yes, of course, and longing for tea," she smiled. He placed her on the blue sofa, nodded to a footman who hastened to bring a silver trolley with beautiful old chased silver, and cups and saucers with the Michieli crest. Viola busied herself with pouring tea. Giorgio looked so troubled and distant that she concentrated on soothing him, and not mentioning her own worries.

He was kind but distant, speaking of introducing her to the staff when she felt ready, and of going for a stroll in the gardens. He asked if she would like to learn to drive a carriage, and accepted, for the present, her gentle refusal.

They talked of the same matters they had always talked of—art and music, Florentine history, England

and her home there. And so the hours went, until dinner. They were served in a smaller dining room—a delicious meal, not one course of which she could remember afterward.

Coffee was served in the smaller drawing room, there they talked idly until he said firmly that she must be weary. She accepted the hint, and went up to her bedroom. Her heart was thumping wildly.

Carmela and an Italian maid came to assist her in undressing. She found her new dresses hanging in the giant wardrobes, new gowns, new dressing gowns, and night-robes. They arrayed her in a robe of white lace and silk, and left her.

She lay in bed with the lights turned low, and finally turned them out completely and buried her face in the soft pillow. He did not come. No door opened, no sound came, no whisper of longing. He did not come.

She was sleepless much of the night, and dawn was lighting the sky when she finally drifted off to a troubled, nightmare-torn slumber. As a consequence, she slept late into the morning, and when she wakened it was noon. A tea tray with now cold tea had been set beside the bed, evidence of Carmela's entry which she had not heard.

When the maid reappeared at Viola's summons, she gave a quick, shy glance at the bed and her mouth tightened disapprovingly, but she said nothing.

Viola dressed and went down to luncheon. Giorgio courteously inquired how she had slept, as though it truly mattered to him.

"Well, thank you," she muttered, and saw him glance at her eyes. She had covered the dark shadows with unaccustomed powder. After luncheon, he took her to his study, and seated her near his large mahogany desk.

"There are some matters of the household to discuss," he said pleasantly. She cast curious looks at the bookshelves, lined with heavy leather-bound volumes, and at the tables covered with papers. "I regret the disarray. My secretary does not come this week. These are matters pertaining to some land." His explanation told her little, she thought.

He sat down then and explained the allowance she would have, paid into a Florentine bank. It was enormous, and she at once protested. "Father has put so much into my account—as you know, Giorgio," she said timidly. "I need no more. I—I feel guilty—"

"Never feel guilty," he said calmly. "You are not guilty, you are the lamb," and then he frowned slightly, and went on swiftly. "I wish you to purchase whatever you require for yourself and the household. The housekeeper will explain the accounts to you. Today I shall introduce you to the staff. If you wish, you may make up the menus, and direct the work."

She scarcely heard him as he went on; her thoughts were busy with his odd remark about the lamb. What lamb? Did he mean that she was a sacrificial lamb?

"Now about our entertaining," he said. "I do not wish to go out much. At this time, it is inconvenient. I shall like you to enjoy dancing and balls, but—perhaps later. We shall invite some friends to our home, and of course I shall take you to visit your father and your sisters in Florence."

She gazed at him, wide-eyed. What did he mean? "I do not have to have balls," she said, with a pang. "But Giorgio, you must not mind your scars. People honor you for them. It should not prevent you from enjoying yourself, at balls and dinners. You do not mind my saying so?"

"You are of a kind nature," he said, without looking at her. "For a reason of my own, I do not wish to attend at this time, and of course you shall not attend without me."

"Of course," she echoed, but felt terribly disappointed. She would not wear the violet gauze, nor the green gown like sea foam, nor many of the other enchanting dresses he had ordered for her.

"One other thing—I shall speak to Carmela Pisani," and he gave a deep sigh. "I am sorry that I cannot permit you to go out without me for a time. You will not go to Florence on any of your expeditions, not for shopping or the museums, or anything else. I do not wish you to venture out without me. This is a strict rule, which I cannot permit you to break. Do you understand? You will obey me?"

She stared at him, aghast. "But I went often before we were married, Giorgio!" she cried. "Oh, please do not deny me."

He seemed to whiten under his tan. "I regret very much I cannot allow it." His voice was curt, his accent pronounced. "I am sorry. There is much in the villa to amuse you. You may read any of these books, see the art in the villa—there are locked cabinets, but I will give you the keys. And we shall visit some homes of my friends, they will enjoy showing you their treasures. For the present, that is all."

He ended the subject, and the grim line of his mouth prevented her further protests. She did not understand at all. And she was hurt. He knew how much she loved to explore Florence. Why did he forbid it?

"Now I shall take you to the music room, you will

like it," he said hastily, and rose to his feet. Rather blindly, she followed him to a room at the back of the villa, a large, magnificent room with parquet floors, carved paneling of rosewood, and the largest piano she had ever seen. He begged her to try it, and rather shyly she played a piece. The sound was exquisite, and he relaxed at her obvious pleasure.

Next to the grand piano was a smaller, older instrument of gilt, with frivolous paintings on the lid and the carved, ornate legs. It was a harpsichord, he told her, and she might play it also. She tried it, and enjoyed the bright tinkling sound.

"This was the ballroom. In the old days, there were many dances here," he said, gazing about absently. "The chandeliers were lit, the doors opened to the gardens and patio. I remember one occasion, when I was eighteen. My parents gave an immense ball for my coming-of-age. There were two hundred guests, spilling into the halls and the drawing rooms. The party went on until morning. My mother wore a gown of rose velvet, with roses in her still-dark hair. My young sister was permitted to remain up until midnight, and she was beautiful in white muslin with a pink sash."

The memory seemed to give him more pain than pleasure, and he turned away impatiently. He pointed out some paintings on the wall, then left her to play, seeming to forget that he had said he would introduce the staff to her.

In the next days, and weeks, she met all the staff, and gradually drew the reins of the household tighter in her hands. The elderly housekeeper was inclined to be eccentric, and Viola thought the staff would be glad of some changes. The chef pondered with her over menus and ventured suggestions. The butler came to her for orders, and seemed to approve of her notions. But she felt she had very little to do. Giorgio was gone much of the day, and when he was home he was frequently closeted with his secretary in the study. She would hear the two men's voices rattling on in crisp Italian for hours. Viola played the piano and the harpsichord, studied Italian with Carmela, carried out her few household duties, and spent too many hours roaming the villa restlessly.

It was a beautiful home, and she was proud when Giorgio invited their first guests. They were three Italian couples, and the conversation was held completely in Italian, since they knew little English. She must study all the harder, she realized, so that she might entertain their guests. When she showed the ladies the changes in some of the rooms, one said, "Ah, now it is beautiful. The villa has been neglected for some time, eh? It is good Giorgio married. He lived with his memories too long."

Viola cherished the slightest remarks the discreet guests made, for they were precious clues to what the man Giorgio was really like. She did not understand him. Carmela made no protest about his orders; she seemed to take for granted that he must have good reasons to forbid them to drive alone into Florence. But Viola felt more and more bewildered and anxious. Something was very wrong, and everyone seemed to comprehend it but her.

And her nights were lonely. Little though she knew of marriage—for her sisters had not enlightened her—she knew that a man and wife slept together, laughed together, kissed each other often, especially when they first married.

However, Giorgio never entered her rooms. He was kind and gentle, but as if to a child. He did not kiss her lips, only her cheek from time to time, impersonally.

He never came to her bed. Never. And growing in her was a longing and a desire to have him touch her, hold her, reassure her that he had married her for some reason beyond revenge.

CHAPTER 7

Giorgio seemed to sense that Viola felt restless and had too much time on her hands. One morning he asked her to come to the library, and there he introduced her to a middle-aged man with a sharp face.

Signor Vannucci was an important official at the bank with which Giorgio dealt, he explained. "I wish the good *Signore* to teach you of finance. You have money which should be invested wisely. Also, it is good for a woman to know how money should be managed, and be able to make decisions. Carmela will remain here with you, and translate whatever you do not understand quite clearly."

Carmela was sent for, and sat near them demurely as they conversed. *Signor* Vannucci came each morning for a week, then twice a week for a month. He talked to Viola of financial matters, first the most simple, then the more complex. Gradually Viola came to understand how money was invested, what stocks meant, how the markets operated. The banker suggested investments for her, and then Giorgio came in and went over them also, and explained his own decisions to Viola. It was interesting, but very strange to Viola. Her father had handled everything for his daughters, only giving the girls money for household expenses.

With their advice, she invested the money her father had given for her dowry, and learned how to understand bank statements and study the gazettes for reports of markets.

When this project was well begun, Giorgio then brought in another younger man, a *Signor* Rustici. He was a shy man, blushing often, but intense in his desire to teach her about philosophy, the great thoughts of the ages. They read portions of English and Italian writers together, and then ventured into the Latin. *Signor* Rustici came on Tuesdays and Fridays, and often remained for luncheon at Viola's invitation, to converse with her and Giorgio. He was indeed an intelligent man, of wide interests.

Viola began to wonder if Giorgio was ashamed of her, that she knew so little, and was determined to educate her so that she could converse with his friends, who were often of great intelligence. But he never told her of his intentions, and she determined to study very hard and make him proud of her.

The days gradually fell into a pattern. June came, and the gardens were vibrant with roses, geraniums, and columbine. The gardeners frequently watered the drying grasses, for the sun seemed to shine constantly.

Viola enjoyed lying out on a lounge in the shade of the patio, gazing at the clipped greens and the glorious colors of the flowers. She listened to the chirping of the birds, and at sunset could hear the bells chiming from Florence in the valley below.

It was one evening as she lay there, watching the rose and orange and pale yellow of the sunset, that she noted a movement in the hedges. Had one of the gardeners lingered late to work in the cool of the evening? She sat up, intent, frowning, as the man came through the hedge. He moved furtively, and was dressed in dark clothing, black, she thought. She could not see his face, only that his hair was dark.

He was staring toward the upper windows of the house. She herself was in the shadow, since the room behind her was not lit. She watched as the man crept forward, keeping to the line of the hedges. He was coming toward her. . . .

Suddenly panicky, she dashed into the villa through the French windows of the drawing room, and into the hallway. The butler, sedately heading toward the kitchens, halted in alarm. "*Signora*—what—"

"A man—in the gardens—he is coming toward the house—" she panted.

Swiftly alert, he called a footman to him, and the two raced out. Carmela ran down the stairs to Viola. "*Signora*, you are not hurt? What is it? I heard the alarm—"

"No, no, but there is a man in the gardens—" They listened, and heard upraised voices, then a shout.

"And the good *Signore* not here," muttered Carmela with a frown. Giorgio had taken a carriage and gone down into Florence on business.

The butler returned, shaking his head. "He departed, the troublemaker, the—" He halted, on seeing Viola's face, taut and strained. "Pardon, *signora*, you will go up to your rooms? We will bring tea to you," he urged her gently.

When Giorgio returned, he listened in silence to

her story. "But who was the man, Giorgio?" she ended.

"I regret so much that you were disturbed. Where there is money, there will always be thieves who wish to steal," he said, and patted her hand. "There is no need for you to be upset. All is well. Guards have been posted."

Somehow she felt that was not the whole story, but Giorgio said no more, and tried to distract her by speaking of a musical group who would come to the villa in a few days to entertain them and their guests.

Viola was reluctant to lie out on the lounge after that, and decided she would take the air on her own balcony, on the floor above. But from there, one afternoon, she noticed a man peering from the trees at the far edge of the gardens. This time she remained still, watching him. He came no closer, perhaps because it was daylight. On the alert now, she again noticed a man one morning, as she glanced from the windows of the library.

Viola felt troubled, and frightened. She was not mistaken; intruders meant to come close. Were they thieves, as Giorgio said? His own men patrolled the gardens, and the road beyond the estate. The gates were always locked at night.

Finally she cornered Carmela, pointing out the watching man to her. "There is that man again, Carmela. Who is he?"

"I do not know, *signora,* I will inform *Signor* Michieli."

Viola caught her hand to draw her back. "No, wait. Watch with me what he does. He never dares come close. I think he is watching what we do here."

Carmela's hand was cold and tense, and Viola was

certain her maid knew more than she said. She bent her efforts to discover what that was.

"Is Giorgio in some danger?" she asked. "Please tell me, Carmela. You have been a good friend to me. Please trust me."

"There—there is little danger, *signora*," Carmela said with unusual reserve, and not looking at Viola. She stared out the windows with her intense black eyes, her olive face troubled. "You must not be unhappy, the *Signore* said so. He has posted guards at all times now."

"But why? What is wrong? It is not the wealth of the family, is it? It is something else? Something from the years of war? Does some enemy shadow Giorgio?"

Finally she forced Carmela to tell her. "But *signora*, you must not fear. However, there is a family from Pisa, and they have been seen here in Florence of recent weeks. A family named the Doria—a bad lot they are! During the war they were accursed enemies of the good *Signore*. For many years they and the Michieli had been on opposite sides. It is a vendetta, you see."

At the woman's words Viola's body seemed to turn as cold as the Alps in winter, with their burden of snow and the biting wind. She put her hand to her breast, and felt the frantic beating of her heart. "Vendetta," she whispered. "That is—that is a blood feud, is it not?"

Carmela nodded, her eyes very troubled as she still stared into the gardens. The man had disappeared beyond the hedges. "*Signora*, the *Signore* your husband did not wish you to be troubled. Yet if you know, you can protect yourself, and be more careful. You must be very careful, for they are bloodthirsty animals, the Doria. All Florence knows of them. One was at your wedding. That is why your husband, he hurry you away."

"But they are not after me, are they? It is Giorgio they—they want—" Viola's voice trembled.

Carmela hesitated, then nodded. "*Si*. They hate him, for he fought bravely, and two of the Doria died. They fought with the French, curse them, and for a time they—how do you say—lived high. Then with our freedom from the forces of the Bonaparte, they lost much. They retreated to their wolf-den in the mountains near Pisa. Now they come out again, snarling devils! How dare they walk the streets of our Florence!"

"And Giorgio is in danger," murmured Viola.

Carmela caught her tone, and turned at once to reassure her. "But your *Signore*, he is a strong, brave man! He will not be caught so easily! Always he takes his men with him, and is armed with the dagger which he uses so well! Do not fear for him, for he fears not for himself. Never was there a man of such courage! All Florence respects him."

But when Carmela had left her, Viola lay back on her lounge and pressed her hands to her face. Giorgio might not fear for himself, but she feared for him. He was in grave danger from men who hated him, who had fought him before, who would do anything, risk anything, to kill him.

She was upset whenever he left the villa now, although she tried to hide it. She was nervous until he returned home. She lost her appetite, and Giorgio was troubled, asking her again and again what was wrong.

"I am all right, Giorgio, please do not mind. Sometimes my appetite disappears in the summertime, in the heat."

"Perhaps I should take you to the mountains," he

said, frowning slightly. "You will miss your English air."

"No, no, I don't want to go back to England," she said hastily. "But perhaps—the mountains—"

"I cannot leave just now, but I could send you with Carmela."

She abruptly refused this, burst into tears, and ran from the room. Giorgio followed her, and tenderly asked what was wrong.

She trembled as he put his hands on her shoulders and tried to study her face. He tipped back her head and studied her expression with a puzzled look.

"What is it, *carina*? You are disturbed? What is wrong?"

"I—I am sometimes worried," she confessed in a low tone. Carmela had asked her not to reveal that she knew about the Doria. It was for her own safety that the maid had told her, but Giorgio had not wished her to know.

"Worried? You are afraid of what?"

"Not—not for myself. For you," she said. "You—have enemies—from the war, I think," she added hastily. "I have seen men watch the villa."

"Oh—that," he said thoughtfully. "But I told you we are well guarded. No, you are not to disturb yourself about me." There was a hard, almost bitter ring to his words, and his face was expressionless. He patted her head, and let her go. "Do not fret. If you are weary of the heat, I will send you to the mountains. I know of a beautiful resort—"

But she refused to go, and restrained her tears this time. She thought if he once made up his mind to send her, he would not relent; no tears would dissuade him. She must be calm, and hide her distress.

The next day Giorgio told her he had received an

invitation from her father and sisters to dinner on Saturday evening. "Would you like to go, *carina*? Are you missing your family?"

She wanted to say that he was her family now, that no one else mattered, but she was too shy to do that. He had shown no indication of wishing her to be a true wife to him.

"I should like to visit them, yes," she said. "That is, if you permit it."

"Permit? Of course I permit it! I had no wish to separate you from your father and sisters." He frowned over the neat, spiky writing which Viola recognized as her sister Eleanor's. "Your sister asks if you might come for the afternoon and remain for the evening. There will be a few friends for dinner. That pleases you?"

"If you wish to go, Giorgio," she told him. He nodded then, suddenly decisive.

"So—we shall go. I have an acquaintance I must see that afternoon. We shall go down to the city about three, I will leave you with your sisters for a friendly gossip, yes? Then I shall return for the evening. It will mean we return late," he added, half to himself, "but we shall be—that is, the roads are good."

Suddenly she knew he was worried about returning in the dark up the unguarded drive to the villa. "We—we don't have to go," she said hurriedly. "Giorgio—I could go some morning—" However, he insisted they go on Saturday.

The days went quickly. When Saturday arrived, Viola debated long over what to wear. Should she be modest in pale muslin? Or glamorous in one of her stunning new frocks, with some of Giorgio's generous gifts of jewelry? Carmela made up her mind for her.

"Your sisters will be arrayed in their best, I think,"

she said shrewdly. "After all, you were the first to marry, and they have different feelings about you, now. So, let your husband be proud of you, eh? The blue silk, eh? Your hair à la Madonna, I shall do it for you, with your beautiful curls piled high on your head. And the poke bonnet of blue with the plumes. And the velvet and silk slippers."

Viola thought she was rather overdressed when Carmela had made her ready. She looked quite unlike herself, almost unrecognizable in the long mirrors with her sophisticated gown and bonnet. And Carmela had urged her to wear the long silver chain with the huge sapphire pendant, her sapphire earrings, and a bracelet, along with her rings.

Giorgio came to the door of the drawing room. "You are ready? Ah, yes, you are splendid," and he looked her over thoughtfully, with a slight smile.

"Carmela said I should dress like this," said Viola defensively. "Do you think I should–"

"Carmela is quite right. You are magnificent, *carina,*" And he nodded to the maid. "Yes, your sisters will be jealous of your appearance. I knew they would be upset when you finally appeared in society."

"The most beautiful of the three," sighed Carmela happily.

"Oh, no, not so beautiful as they are!" said Viola, shocked. "No one could outshine Eleanor, she is so stunning. And Bernice draws all eyes when she is gowned and coiffed."

"They will look at *you* tonight," her husband predicted, and helped her adjust the pelisse of blue silk over her shoulders.

Viola received a more unpleasant shock when they went out to the carriage. Two grooms were up on the driving seat, and about the carriage were positioned six horsemen in Michieli livery, all set to accompany them. She glanced up at Giorgio apprehensively. His face was expressionless.

"Some will remain with you at your father's house. Others will come with me," he said brusquely. "Do not argue. Your jewels are a temptation."

"Oh—I shall take them off," she said weakly, her hand on the sapphire pendant.

"Not at all. We merely take precautions," said Giorgio smoothly, and helped her into the carriage.

So he still persisted in trying to make her think that it was thieves that concerned him. Her pleasure in the day and the outing were dimmed. The sun shone brightly, the road down to Florence wound in and out of beautiful vistas, but she saw little. Giorgio was in grave danger.

Sir Anthony came out to greet them as though he had been watching for them. He waited until Giorgio had helped Viola down, then came to kiss her cheek warmly and clasp her to him. "My dear, it has been too long since we have had the pleasure of your company. I thought your husband meant to keep you entirely to himself," he said, in smiling reproach.

"We have been so busy," said Viola, pleased at her father's emotions. At times she had thought he cared little for her. "You will be amazed at the lessons I am learning, all about finance and philosophy and Latin!"

"Good heavens above," he said mildly. He urged them indoors out of the hot sun, and sent for the older girls. They soon came and exclaimed over Viola, over her gown and jewels, and asked how she did.

Giorgio soon excused himself and went off. The girls and their father chatted comfortably all afternoon. They had much to ask about her new home, and whether she was comfortable and happy.

"You seem thinner," said her father critically. "The girls are minding the heat. But I thought in the hills you would be better off."

"It is the heat," she said quickly. "But I shall adjust to it. And there is often a breeze in the gardens."

"I may have to send the girls back to England. I could pay for a chaperone for them," her father said, frowning. "Perhaps you might join them for the summer."

"No, no, I don't want to leave. Please say nothing to Giorgio."

Giorgio returned about seven, looking rather weary. Viola hastened to bring him a glass of wine, and the girls watched critically as he smiled slightly and thanked her. Soon after, their other guests arrived. To Viola's dismay, Reginald Selby and Niccolo Leopardo were among the number.

Giorgio's manner was chilly but courteous. They could not fault his manners. Viola whispered later to Eleanor, "How could you? You know Giorgio does not care for them!"

"Oh, what does it matter? The wars are over, they should learn to be friendly. My dear, you should know that in diplomatic circles, it pays to be friends with everyone," said Eleanor earnestly. She patted Viola's cheek. "We shall come up to you soon for a real conversation, since your husband does not allow you out alone."

Now, how had she learned that? Viola wondered. And between feeling on edge around the two men she disliked, and watching Giorgio's expressions, she began to wish they could go home, and be quite alone. Reginald Selby was courteous also, but his green eyes were like ice chips, and Niccolo Leopardo was frigid. They talked to Giorgio, but only in generalities, watching him like two great, uneasy cats, thought Viola.

Sir Anthony was too much the diplomat to allow any silences or awkward topics to be introduced. The evening flowed smoothly along. Viola was too agitated to note the food or drinks; she merely picked at her plate.

Giorgio and Viola were the last to leave, and Eleanor insisted on a final intimate talk before they departed. It was well past midnight when they at last arose.

Eleanor seemed more at ease with her brother-in-law now. And Viola knew her sister was determined to make a name for herself as a hostess; no doubt Eleanor had realized Giorgio could be considered an asset. She dared to say, rather pertly, as they gathered up their cloaks and Viola's bonnet, "Giorgio, will you tell me what caused you to choose little Viola as your wife, rather than one of us?" Her laughing gesture included Bernice and herself.

Sir Anthony threw Eleanor a sharp look, and Giorgio's mouth curved in an ironic smile.

Viola was holding her breath, fearing some angry blast. But Giorgio finally said, "I had several reasons, and considered the matter very carefully. However, you might be interested in one reason—I decided that Viola would be the one most missed by all of you."

There was a stunned silence from them all. Bernice finally broke it, in an incredulous, laughing voice. "Missed by us? Viola? But she was always at home! She had not come out, she has few social graces—I don't understand!"

"I think you are beginning to understand," said Giorgio, and bade them a firm good-night.

CHAPTER 8

Viola longed to ask Giorgio what he had meant by his remark. And she would dearly love to know what other reasons he had had for marrying her. But she did not dare bring up the topic.

Though he was usually gentle and considerate with her, he could speak with such harsh, biting cynicism that she dreaded bringing on any such speech. The war years had given him a hardness which nothing would soften. She had listened to him as he spoke with her father, and sometimes his view of society, or politics, or the motives of officials would bring a frown to Sir Anthony's brow. Giorgio seemed to trust few men now, and she could not blame him.

Wistfully, she hoped to soften him, but he showed no signs of wishing any more intimate relations between them. He came to her drawing room only when he wished to approve a gown, and never to her bedroom.

Each morning she went out with a gardener and cut fresh flowers, filling the vases and bowls of the villa with vivid roses, pink and blue columbine, even fresh stalks of fragrant shrubs, which scented the house delicately. She practiced music he seemed to enjoy, and lived for the few evenings when he seemed to wish to sit and listen to her playing. She consulted the chef anxiously, tried new recipes, watched for Giorgio's reactions, and was happy when he approved of anything.

Yet they drew no closer, she felt, than host and guest, or employer and housekeeper! He worked hard, but told her nothing of his work. She told him of her lessons, and occasionally they discussed philosophy or finance, or he would listen while she carefully read aloud in Italian.

About a week later, Eleanor and Bernice came up to the villa. Viola had invited them, and they came partly from curiosity, she knew. They arrived about two, and would remain until six, when Giorgio would arrive home. He said vaguely that he would, at a later time, invite them for an evening of music with some of his Italian friends.

"However, I think they might be uncomfortable," he added. "Your sisters do not trouble to learn Italian, I believe. They might do well to do so. I understand Sir Anthony may remain another six months."

"Oh, I hope he does," she said eagerly. "Though—does his mission proceed badly, Giorgio?"

He gave her the cynical smile she disliked. "It goes slowly, it may fail," he said harshly. "The Florentines have long memories, as I have troubled to inform your father. They recall the war years, and they are not entirely sure of his—shall I say, integrity?"

About to protest, she recalled his own plight, and she flushed deeply and was silent, hanging her head.

Giorgio put out his hand and touched her hair gently, his fingers light on the soft curls.

"Do not fret over this," he said. "If the Florentines decide that English wool is a good exchange for Italian silks, the deals will eventually go through. After all, despite the fine talk of exchange of trade and improved diplomatic relations, it is a hardheaded matter for merchants. And Florentines were bankers to the world while the British were still running about half-naked with furs about their middles!"

"Giorgio!" she said, completely surprised. He gave a short, gruff laugh, and seemed surprised at himself.

"It is true. You must read more history," he teased her, and turned the subject. "You think the British are so civilized and advanced, yet they are several centuries behind the Italians. Roman civilization is more than two thousand years old, and at that time the British lived in swamps and on islands, fighting each other with sticks."

She smiled reluctantly. "I fear you are right." And the subject went far from the affairs of her father. But his words had stung. Her father's integrity was in question, and probably her own. Oh, if only she could prove to Giorgio that she was to be trusted! Perhaps that was why he kept aloof from her. Yet—yet he had married her.

Her sisters arrived in their carriage, escorted by two servants. Eleanor and Bernice were seated in the smaller drawing room, comfortably conversing while their sharp eyes took in every luxurious detail.

Eleanor was radiant in crimson trimmed with golden flounces; her bonnet was bordered with real gold braid. Bernice wore her favorite blue-green silk, the shirred bonnet set back from her dark blond hair.

Yet they gazed with envy at Viola in her violet silk, with the amethysts at her throat and her wrist.

"We have heard since your wedding that Giorgio is immensely wealthy," Bernice said rather spitefully. "Why in heaven's name didn't he say so at the time?"

"And refusing to go to balls and dinners!" added Eleanor. "We hear that ordinarily he goes out often, and was frequently seen with one Florentine woman or another, the most beautiful women imaginable!"

Viola did not allow her own bewilderment to show on her face. "Giorgio has his own reasons. I do not question him," she murmured.

This docile wifely reply did not satisfy her sisters. Eleanor looked sharply from the low bowl of white Chinese porcelain in which Viola had set two water lilies with hearts of gold, to an ivory figurine near it, to the priceless tapestry behind the cream satin sofa. "I cannot understand it. He said people shrank from his scars. From what I hear, he is courted by all the best families. So why did he marry you, of all people?"

There was a sharp sting of malice behind the words. Viola shrank from them. With all her heart she longed to be able to assert that Giorgio had married her because he loved her. But he did not. He was kind and gentle, but he showed no signs of loving her. He had not even made her his real wife. Was he perhaps planning some subtle revenge, something terrible he had not yet revealed to her? A cool wind seemed to pass through the dim room, and freeze her heart. Oh, surely, surely, he would not do that!

To her relief, the butler entered, wheeling the silver tea trolley. She smiled, and gestured for it to be placed before her. The girls eyed the tray greedily, as much for the delicate porcelain with the purple and gold decoration, and the silver tea service, as for the cakes deliciously arrayed. They watched in silence as the butler bent to help Viola serve, and proceeded grandly from one to the other, helping them choose from the tiny sandwiches and pastries with swirls of chocolate, almond paste, and whipped cream.

After the butler had left the room, Eleanor let out a sigh. "Oh, to have someone like that! Do you know, the chef left but a week after your wedding! He was very insulting, he said he could not understand a word I said, and he would not remain to wait upon the middle classes! I was furious!"

"Oh, dear!" Viola stared at her sister. "He left? But he was an excellent chef, temperamental, but very good. I had not known—"

"Your precious Giorgio helped him obtain another post, with some titled friends of his," added Bernice, leaning back, with a luxurious sigh, into the puffed cushions at her back. "Oh, this cream cake is—mmmmmm—Our new chef won't last long, I can tell. Eleanor is merely enduring him until she finds someone better. Did you not notice the soup the evening you came? Terribly salty!"

Eleanor went on bitterly, "And I spend half my days at the markets, with a housekeeper who pretends not to understand my English! Father said we should have learned Italian, but why should I? They can learn English!"

"If you remain longer, you really should make the attempt," Viola said gently.

Two pairs of suspicious eyes flew to hers. "Longer? What do you know of that?" Eleanor demanded. "Has Father been here? Did you know he hasn't yet obtained an agreement to take back to London?"

"Oh, hasn't he?" murmured Viola. "But this means

you will stay for a few more months, doesn't it? I dread the day you must return. I shall miss you." Even as she said the words, she knew they were no longer true. She did not miss her home or her sisters, and her father only a little. Giorgio was her life now. She had made a few friends among the Italian ladies, and next week two of them were coming to call. She looked forward to becoming closer to the bright young wife of an attorney, and the older, wise wife of a nobleman.

Eleanor tried to question Viola sharply about what Giorgio might know, but Viola turned away her questions, and said sympathetically, "But tell me about the servants. Only the chef has left, I hope?"

"As if that were the half of it," sighed Bernice. "The maid left, and we have had the task of training another. Also Papa found it difficult to find another English girl, and we had to get some Irish wench, who is impertinent and always answers back! But Papa says we must keep her, for he won't endure the trouble of getting another girl! Oh, I long to return to London, where the servants are glad to have their positions, and do what is told without snapping at one!"

"And the markets!" added Eleanor, her mouth drooping. "Oh, Viola, to have to smell the fish, and those great hunks of meat dripping blood in the shops! I cannot stand it much longer! I told Papa he must force the housekeeper to do more. He flings up his hands, and says the villa is my concern, he has enough to worry about. So we must endure insolence from the footmen, and trotting about in the heat—"

Viola tried to sympathize, but she could not help recalling the days when she did all that work, and they had nothing to think about but a hair-style, a new gown, the dinner that evening, the gossip they had heard the evening before.

Presently they inquired what she did all day. Their eyebrows were raised sharply when she told them of her lessons. "Money and its management?" asked Bernice, sniffing. "I should refuse! Giorgio ought to take time to do all that."

"I find it quite fascinating," said Viola with composure. "Now I can understand the gazettes from London. Giorgio brings the latest newspapers from Florence, and all the books I could want. In addition he had some precious volumes in his own library, of art and music and biography. I never have enough time to read all I want to."

"You haven't had to do any work for a time, I can tell," sighed Bernice. "We had to do the cooking for a week, when the chef went off to a funeral, can you imagine it? And sometimes I have to do my own hair, and wash out a few things."

Viola suppressed a smile, recalling the times she had waited on them. "Truly, Giorgio does spoil me," she said innocently. "With all the servants about, it is a struggle to be allowed to do a little cooking. If I did not insist, Giorgio would never approve. But he allows me to do as I wish."

It was wicked, but she loved their expressions as she said this. After that, she grew ashamed of herself, and begged them to tell her where they had gone, what great ladies they had visited, with whom they had danced, who had called. This entertained them until six, when Giorgio returned, and came to greet them.

After they had taken their departure, Giorgio asked, as though idly, "Of what did you speak all the afternoon? They looked very pleased with themselves."

"Oh—yes, I think they are happy in the main. However, they have had some trouble keeping servants. The chef departed."

"I noticed, the evening we had dinner there," said Giorgio blandly, but with a gleam in his eyes.

About to remind him that Eleanor had said he himself had obtained another position for the chef, Viola swallowed the words. "Did your day go successfully?" she managed.

"Well, thank you." Giorgio rose, and went to the silver tray the butler had left, with a bottle of sherry and two delicate glasses. He poured the amber liquid and brought a glass to her. She accepted it, and he delicately clinked his glass with hers.

"To your health." He raised the glass to her.

"And to yours, Giorgio. Your health and happiness," she said deliberately, and ignored the rising of his dark eyebrows. She sipped at the dry sherry, savoring its delightful bouquet. Giorgio had a fine taste in wines, and would have only the best served. She studied the liquid swirling in her slim glass, the crystal glinting. What topic was safe to discuss with him tonight? He seemed on edge, as though eager to argue, to strike out verbally. He was rarely thus with her.

"It is two hours until dinner," she said finally. "If you are not too weary, do you have the patience to listen to my efforts with the harpsichord?"

He gave her an absent smile, relenting from his harshness. "Never too weary for that, my dear. Shall we go into the other room?"

The butler followed at once with the silver tray and sherry. In the huge music room, Viola seated herself on the plush piano stool, in front of the harpsichord, and waited for Giorgio to seat himself in a blue plush chair near the instrument. The butler brought a small table to him, and set the silver tray beside him. Giorgio filled another glass, and looked questioningly at Viola.

"You will have more sherry, my dear?"

"No, thank you. Not now." And she began to play softly, a gentle melody that went on and on, like a brook singing to itself, weaving in, out, and around the tune. She had the satisfaction of seeing him set down the half-empty glass, lean his dark head against the velvet back of the chair, and close his eyes. The scarred face began to relax.

She played for more than an hour, one piece after another. Sometimes he kept his eyes closed. Another time, she would be aware of his eyes gazing steadily at her profile as she bent to the keys. Finally she paused.

"Very beautiful, *carina,*" he said. "But I tire you with all this. I shall go and change for dinner. Will you wear the blue silk I like, and the sapphires?"

"Of course," she said, and jumped up, smiling radiantly at him. So he did notice what she wore, and enjoyed seeing her in the beautiful gowns he had purchased for her. "And I—I would like to thank you for the new gowns that arrived today. You are too extravagant with me! And just the colors that I like so much."

He had risen, and put one finger on her soft cheek, in a light caress. "It is my pleasure," he said. "I enjoy seeing you look so stunning that all my friends envy me. But an evening alone with you will be most pleasant. I am weary of people. Sometimes I would be a hermit in a cave, and never see a person from one year to the next!"

She gazed up at him, her eyes wide with bewilderment. Did he mean he was tired of her also? His home had been his own until he brought her to it; he could be alone in his study or any room he chose. Did she trouble him?

"Do I—bother you?" she blurted out, in a low tone. "Would you rather I had not married—"

The finger moved to close her mouth gently. "I did not say that, nor think it, *amoretta*," he said swiftly. Then he frowned. "Go and change for dinner, or the chef will be cross with us, eh?" And he took her shoulders and turned her to the door. Together they went up the stairs to their rooms, and he nodded and left her at the door of her drawing room.

Carmela was waiting for her, and quickly helped her change to the blue silk brocade with the low neck, which showed her slim white throat and the gentle rise of her bosom. It was not a daring gown, but it was lower than the ones she had owned before her marriage. The sapphire pendant swung against her breasts, magnificent with its dark blue flame. She added the sapphire eardrops, the slim bracelet, and studied her ring thoughtfully. What did their marriage mean to Giorgio? Had he meant to take his revenge, then wearied of the idea, or repented it, and found himself left with a young female who bored him?

She was in the drawing room before him. The butler announced dinner a few minutes after Giorgio came down, fine in a blue silk suit. They went in together to the small dining room, and she sat at his right, as she had so often. But this evening the silence stretched for long minutes, until they rose and went to the small drawing room for their coffee.

Giorgio sat near the fire, for the stone villa was sometimes chilly on a summer evening. He stretched out his legs, set aside the coffee cup and spoke to the butler, who at once produced a bottle of brandy and a graceful snifter.

"Would you like some brandy, Viola?" asked Giorgio, although he knew she did not like the stuff.

"No, thank you." She watched the butler leave the room, and sipped a little of her coffee. Giorgio was tired, but more than that, she sensed he was sick at heart. Something troubled him deeply, something he could neither conquer nor expel from his mind.

Deliberately daring, she took a plump blue cushion from behind her and rose. Giorgio was staring intently at the fire and did not notice her until she came over to him.

"I like to sit on the floor near the fire," she said with a smile, and before he could rise, she dropped the cushion to the floor, and curled up gracefully on it, her slim legs bent under her skirts. She sat close to him, at his feet. "This reminds me of times in London, when the fog rolled in, and the cold dampness would make us huddle before the fires. Sometimes we would have our supper in the nursery before the fire, and Eleanor would let me sit like this to eat."

From the corner of her eye, awaiting his reaction to her move, she saw his tanned, scarred hand move, then hesitate. Then he touched her head so softly she scarcely felt the touch. But in every fiber of her being, she knew his hand was there.

After a pause, she said, "The London winters were so cold. Sometimes the girls would not want to go out. But I would run out in my blue cloak, and slide up and down the paths in the garden, where the ice had formed. Oh, the poor flowers, they would become so dark and wilted. I can scarce believe I am in a country where the flowers bloom all year round."

The fingers moved, and slid down her warm cheek. "And you do not regret that you live in my sunny Florence?" he whispered.

She dared to lean her cheek closer to his hand, and settled herself against his knee. He stiffened, and she wondered if he would push her away. "Regret? I love it more and more," she said simply.

There was a long silence between them. The fire crackled, and his fingers smoothed her cheek again and again.

Finally he spoke. "I remember evenings like this, summer and winter, when my parents and my sister and I were about the fire. We would talk, and laugh, and sing. I liked company, but it was best when we were alone, the four of us. Then Papa would speak of the future, and his plans for us, and—"

He halted abruptly, as though the words caught in his throat.

"What did your Papa plan for you, Giorgio?" she dared to ask. "You see, Papa did not plan for us. He expected us to marry, and for our husbands to bear with our extravagant ways, so he used to say." She laughed a little. "But boys are different. Did he wish you to go into trade? What work did he do?"

He hesitated, and she held her breath. Had she gone too far? Would he rise, and coldly inform her it was none of her concern?

The fingers continued to caress her absently. "My father was a silk merchant, as I am," he confided abruptly. "He had many silk factories about Tuscany. He planned to enlarge the works, and do more of the designing for the brocades and the fabrics he enjoyed.

Like me, he was an artist, but always he had the business head as well, shrewd and careful."

She scarcely dared to breathe. So this was what Giorgio did all day! And he had never told her. Did he think she would be ashamed that he was in trade? But she was not of noble birth, although her father had earned a knighthood for his diplomatic successes. Giorgio mused on, telling her a little about his work, and about the old days when his father had planned many of the designs. "During the war, the work almost halted, but many of the designers and craftsmen were still in Florence when I reopened the factories once more. We have only three factories now, but that is enough. The gown you wear is made of silk from our own place." There was pride in his tone.

"Oh, no wonder you know so much about dresses, and how to design them. My wedding dress–I adored it, Giorgio. Never did a girl have such a beautiful wedding gown. And this dress–is the silk from your factories?"

Encouraged, he talked more, and his voice grew warmer and more intimate there in the dimness, with only the fire to give light, along with a few candles on the table behind them. He ignored his brandy glass, as he talked on and on of the work, of his parents, even of his beloved younger sister. And somehow in the darkness, unable to see his face, but knowing the touch of his fingers, Viola felt closer to him than she ever had.

CHAPTER 9

Giorgio withdrew into himself after that evening. Yet Viola felt she had made progress in growing closer to him. Oh, it might be a long, hard struggle, but it was one she was determined to win. Giorgio had much bitterness in him, but she was anxious to win him back to happiness once more. He deserved the best, the most that life had to give. And she was content to remain at home with him in the evening. She needed no one else to complete her joy. She was not accustomed to much merriment, so she did not miss it, or long for what she had never had.

A few evenings later, on a warm night in mid-June, Giorgio told her they would go out the following afternoon for a concert at the home of a friend who lived in a private palace about two miles from their villa. "It is a splendid home," he said absently. "You will enjoy it. And the concert. A piano and violin, I believe. They were most cordial, Viola. Will you be ready at three o'clock?"

"Of course, Giorgio, as you wish," she said simply. His gaze rested on her face. Sometimes he seemed to stare at her as though seeing through her, beyond her. She wondered if he even realized that he stared.

"Perhaps you will wear the pale green gown I ordered for you recently. You will look like spring itself," and he smiled faintly.

She did as he asked, and came down to the drawing room early the next afternoon. Standing on tiptoe, she looked in the gilded mirror over the mantel to survey her hair.

He came in behind her as she anxiously patted a curl into place, and lightly put his hands on her shoulders. He turned her about, and studied her up and down.

She colored a little. "Do—do I look all right?"

"You look beautiful. Everyone will envy me," he said.

She wished he would put his lips to her cheek, even in the absentminded caress he sometimes gave her. But he merely placed the white shawl about her shoulders, and gave her his arm as they walked to the carriage.

As the coach wound up the hills, he spoke casually of the persons she would meet. "There is Count Salviati. He is the uncle of our host, Count Alessandro Peruzzi. You already know Countess Lucia, his wife."

"Oh, yes, she was most kind at the dinner last week." She had liked the young countess, her gaiety, her sweetness, her smart appearance. She had not acted as though Viola were not good enough for Giorgio, but had treated her as the wife of a loved friend.

Giorgio nodded, and went on to speak of others. She memorized the names, murmured them after him so she would recall them more easily. He was gazing behind them, twisting about in his seat, when she suddenly realized the sound of approaching hoofbeats was becoming louder.

A man in dark clothing, dressed like a workman, had come up on a cob of a horse. He raised his hand to his forehead respectfully, and leaned down to the carriage which Giorgio had ordered to be pulled up. Giorgio's outriders drew about the carriage protectively as the workman handed Giorgio a note.

He frowned, tore open the note, and read it swiftly. "*Per Dio*," he swore softly. "They can do nothing right unless I am there. No, no, this cannot—Viola, forgive me. I must go back to Florence for about an hour or two. I will return swiftly. You must go ahead to the villa, make my deepest apologies to our hostess, and await me. Benito, give me your horse. You take my place in the carriage, and look after my wife."

The exchange was quickly made. Giorgio took one of the men with him, and strictly ordered the others to take every precaution in escorting Viola. Then he was on his way. Benito was abject when he saw Viola's disappointment.

"It is too bad, *ma donna*," the trusted servant said, "but the *Signore* is most efficient. He must tend to his business, eh?"

"Yes, yes, and he said he will come quickly," she replied with only a small sigh of regret. The carriage presently drew up before the entrance to a magnificent villa, set like a jewel in the midst of elaborate clipped hedges, silk-smooth grass, and flower beds. As she mounted the crumbling steps lined with statues of gods and goddesses, Benito was beside her, and another man behind her. She was greeted by her hostess just at the entrance of the palace.

"Come in, my dearest Viola! But where is our

naughty Giorgio?" Her lilting voice was a complement to her pretty face, thought Viola, gazing at the woman's smooth, magnolia-petal complexion, the jet-black hair in soft waves about the oval of her face.

Viola presented Giorgio's regrets, then greeted Lucia's husband Alessandro. He smiled at her warmly, pressed her hand, and brought her to meet his uncle, Count Salviati. There were other guests, a huge crowd, she thought forlornly, looking at the more than fifty people gathered in the drawing room and on the terrace overlooking the gardens.

She wished Giorgio were beside her. She had met some of the guests before, but others were strangers; Giorgio would have known them all. She was intensely aware of the critical looks directed at her, the murmurs of curiosity. She knew some of his friends disapproved of her youth, and of the fact that she was English.

Count Alessandro could not have been more courteous, but he was soon called away to his duties. Viola spoke to one couple, and conversed with an older lady whom she admired. It was while she was talking with the white-haired countess that she heard the voices behind them.

"So that is the girl he married. Such a child! I hear he felt sorry for her, that is the story."

The voice was cool and cutting, the accent Neapolitan. She was beginning to recognize the various accents now. The response was equally catty. "Merely the youngest daughter of some British person, not even noble. Giorgio could have done so well! One wonders what Maria Luisa thinks of it! She was confident she would marry him. She even spoke of spending the winters in Switzerland when they were married!"

"Poor Maria Luisa, she minds the heat. But she minds even more the desertion of her devoted Giorgio!" The two women laughed softly. "One hears she has not left Florence all summer. Does she think the ill-advised marriage might break up sooner with her nearby?"

The voices lowered. "I think I saw her with him one evening at a café. I know it was Giorgio, and from behind it looked to be Maria Luisa. That glorious chestnut hair, her erect carriage—how much more suitable she would have been! No money, but of the nobility!"

The dear old countess was partially deaf; from her serene expression as she watched the guests around them, Viola guessed she did not hear the conversation at their backs. But Viola, in the long pause in her own conversation, heard them only too well.

They moved away, leaving her with her agonized thoughts. Giorgio and a beautiful noble Italian woman—whom he would have married if he had not been carried away with thoughts of revenge! Was that what had gone wrong with Viola's marriage? He had married her for revenge, only to find that he had wrecked his own hopes for happiness with—Maria Luisa. She remembered the woman. They had met twice already. She was seen everywhere, and Giorgio had spoken with her at the villa where they had dined last week, Viola remembered now. The tall, beautiful woman with the carriage of a duchess or a queen. She had worn a dramatic white brocade gown with a modest strand of pearls. Her face has been mobile and expressive as she gazed up at Giorgio. Yes, Viola had noticed her well.

Countess Lucia beckoned them into another room, and they trooped after her to seat themselves on little chairs with yellow-brocaded seats. Above them the ceiling was painted pale blue with white clouds drifting across its serene expanse. White curtains were draped in lavish folds about each window, shutting out the sun and heat, leaving the interior dim and cool. The floors were of darkly shining parquet, with no rugs to muffle the sound of the magnificent grand piano and the violin which would come alive in the hands of the musician. The musicians bowed, waited for silence, and began.

Ordinarily Viola would have loved the concert. Now, sitting alone in the corner where her misery had sent her, she could scarcely hear. The music flowed and ceased, the guests applauded and waited politely for the next selection. Giorgio did not come.

The old countess nodded her white head and tapped her little black-slippered foot in time to the lively music of a dance. Viola listened with a fixed smile, and longed for the ordeal to be over. Where was Giorgio?

She glanced warily about the room, studying the heads of the guests—black curls, crisp masculine heads, high-piled white heads; she lingered over any chestnut. But the woman Maria Luisa was not there. Nor was Giorgio. And inevitably jealousy forced Viola to wonder if they were together.

Had Maria Luisa dared to send him a note to ask her to come? Was that why Benito had felt so sorry for her? Was that why Giorgio had rushed off? Could any work have drawn him from her side, when he had promised to attend a concert at the home of important people?

Surely he would not have so insulted their hosts! Yet—yet if Giorgio were becoming desperate. . . . Did he regret their marriage? Did he plan with Maria Luisa how to end it?

Suddenly Viola remembered something she had heard. In the Catholic Church, if a marriage had not been consummated, there could be an annulment. Divorce was heavily frowned upon, but annulments could be granted, the marriage dissolved, where there was sufficient cause.

She felt icy-cold there in the warm room. Her little hands clutched each other spasmodically. Her mind went round and round frantically. Could it be true? Was Giorgio with that woman?

She heard nothing else of the concert. Her thoughts were turned inward, in suffering so intense that she knew no fact but one. She loved Giorgio, and to leave him would be death. When had she begun to love him? She could not be sure, but felt with all her soul that it had begun at the moment when she had approached the low wall and seen his scarred face, heard him speak to her and call her "*ma donna.*"

The music finally ended. Dazed, she stood up and went to her hostess. She managed to smile and make her apologies. "I must return home, and see that Giorgio is all right," she said, when her hostess protested that she must remain for tea. Regretfully, they allowed her to go.

Benito was on the alert, and sprang up when he saw her appear in the front door. The others waited near the carriage. He escorted her down the darkened steps, for it was dusk now, and they walked past the bushes and hedges, past the fragrant scents of the gardens, the jasmine, the orange-blossoms, the roses, the shy violets.

The steps were dark there in the hedges, and Benito held one of her arms and kept his other hand to his dagger, watching alertly. She was dazed, she could not think. She only wished to be with Giorgio, she could not wait to reach the carriage.

There was a rustle, a sound. . . .

Benito gave a shout. But someone had sprung at Viola, and deep into her shoulder was plunged a cold knife, with a slicing movement which ripped her silken dress. There was no pain as he drew it out, no feeling at all but surprise. She staggered, holding her arm instinctively, as Benito turned to meet the shadowy figures.

Others sprang from near the carriage. They were fighting there in the dusk, the purple and gold liveried servants of the Michieli struggling with—was it half a dozen men? Dark forms grunting, panting, knives glittering in the dusk.

A blow was struck, Benito went down, and another purple and gold clad man sprang near Viola to protect her. The men's shouting caused lights to spring up in the villa. "Ho—what is it—who is there? Bring lights—ho—to the rescue—ho there!"

The sounds were growing dim. Viola sank to the steps, clutching at the statue of a goddess who seemed to peer down at her with cold eyes.

Then Giorgio was there, shouting, fighting with a man who tried to grasp him. Viola watched, but her eyes were heavy, and blood streamed from between her fingers clasped to her shoulder.

Blood—on her pretty green dress—blood. . . .

She crumpled up, and knew nothing more, as the darkness flowed mercifully over her.

CHAPTER 10

Sometimes all was blackness, and sometimes it was gray. In the gloom figures struggled, and knives flashed, and Viola cried out, jerking convulsively. Then pain would strike through her, and she felt weak and sick. She would sink down into the blackness again, and know nothing more.

Several times she heard Giorgio's voice, and he seemed to be murmuring caressingly to her. It must be her imagination, for he never used such words of love to her. "Dearest, darling, be very still and quiet, calm yourself. There is nothing to fear, my adored one," he murmured in Italian. "*Amoretta, amore mia,* lie gently in my arms. Do not be afraid."

She tried to answer him, but the effort was too great. Her tongue was thick and dry, her throat choked. But his touch soothed her—or was this a waking dream? She did not know the difference any longer.

Finally she wakened completely, and opened her

eyes to find herself in her own bed. She was lying on her side, and the first thing she saw was a white porcelain bowl filled with violets. How pretty, she thought dimly, violets, her favorite flower. Had Giorgio sent them to her? She turned slowly, painfully. Her left arm ached with a fierce dulling pain, as though she had felt that ache for a long time.

On the tall, carved post at the foot of the bed, the sea dragons rioted about the wood. The canopy had been drawn back to allow fresh air from the open French windows to flow about her. She blinked at the narrow streams of sunlight. Something had happened in the darkness, something horrible and frightening.

Memory began to flood back. She moaned a little as she recalled the darkness, the crumbling steps, the men who had come like fantastic, horrible figures out of the night to strike with shining daggers. She put her hand to her head, felt it caught and held in strong grip.

Giorgio was bending over her, his face anxious. "Viola, *cara,* you are awake at last?" he asked frantically. "Dearest, do you know me?"

What an odd question. She knew him as she knew her own heart. Her wide gray eyes studied his face. Then she noticed the stubble of beard on his face, the red rims about his eyes. He looked anxious and worn to the bone.

"Giorgio," she muttered, and clung to his hand with both her own. "You are here, you are here."

"Yes, *cara,* I am here. How do you feel?"

She was conscious of the heat of fever, the pain in her left shoulder, but the mists were clearing from her brain. "My shoulder—hurts. Oh, Giorgio—you—you came back." Weakly she began to cry.

He sat down on the bed, slipped his arm about her,

and drew her up into his arms. Safely held to his lean strength, she felt comforted, and clung to his hand as he soothed her with his close arms and his soft voice.

"You are all right, you are here, my Viola. They will not harm you. The nightmares are over, my love. There, darling, rest against your Giorgio, and be calm." His lips touched her hot forehead, he held her hands comfortingly, and with her face resting against his chest, she could hear his heart beating against her ear.

The tears ceased, and she drew a great sigh. "I had such horrible dreams. I dreamed you went away," she murmured. "And they—in the darkness—"

"Yes, yes, they are gone, quite gone. They will never come near you again, by my faith," he said fiercely. "How dared they attack you, my little angel, who never hurt anyone."

She felt him tremble with anger, and she curled closer to him and shut her eyes contentedly. He was holding her, they could not come.

She slept again, the deep sleep of healing, although nightmares lingered on the edges of her dreams. But always Giorgio was there, soothing her, comforting her, and the horrors sank away once more.

She wakened again as the evening sun was sinking, leaving streaks of pink, soft orange, and crimson across the sky. From the open French windows came the sound of the bells pealing in Florence, in the valley below. She lay listening to them, thinking of the great marble cathedral, and the soft, seashell colors of the campanile beside it. All the glories of Florence.

Carmela stirred beside her, and bent forward, her kindly face concerned. "Ah, you waken, Miss Viola! I will call the *Signore*!" and she went swiftly away before Viola could stop her.

Giorgio returned, wearing a robe, obviously roused from sleep. He looked refreshed, and considerably less frantic. He came to the bed and sat carefully beside her, reaching for her hand. She clasped it, feeling his strength flowing into her, and managed a smile.

"You are better, Viola. Your eyes are clear and bright. How do you feel now?" His free hand smoothed back the tumbled blond curls from her face.

How gentle he was with her, how she loved his touch. "Better, not so warm," she managed to say, "How—how long have I slept?"

"No matter, two days and nights," he said. "The doctor comes again tomorrow morning. Your shoulder—there is not so much pain?" Lightly he touched her neck near the great white bandages that muffled her shoulder and arm.

"No, there is not so much pain." She did not tell him she could not move for fear of bringing on the shooting pain that slashed through her dull aching. "You—you are all right, Giorgio?" She studied him anxiously.

"Not a scratch," he assured her.

She began to remember more. "Benito—he—he went down. Is he—"

"His hard head took most of it," said Giorgio, patting her hand lightly. "He is more concerned about you, and in despair that he did not protect you. He hangs about the kitchens, waiting for any word of you. What shall I tell him tonight?"

"Please thank him for his great care of me. It was not his fault—so many of them—" She shuddered, and he frowned.

"Do not try to speak any more. I wish you to eat

something this evening, then rest again. You will have a little egg custard, some tea?"

Her lips were dry, her throat as though stuffed with cotton. She nodded. "Tea," she said weakly. Carmela hastened from the room to bring a tray.

After she had eaten, she slept again, with Giorgio beside her. He must sit there for hours, she thought, for whenever she wakened, he was there, clasping her hand in his strong fingers.

The doctor came in the morning, took off the huge bandages, and examined the wound. He was a small, alert, middle-aged man, who spoke in jerky syllables. He nodded several times, and smiled at Viola. "You will do, you will do," he said, and put on a lighter bandage. He would come again the next day, he assured her.

Giorgio told her that her father had sent a man every day to inquire how she did, and her sisters were most alarmed. They sent flowers the third day, and a note from them all with their fervent messages for her safe recovery.

"Your father will call when I allow it," he said. "He is most anxious to see you. Also the Count and Countess Peruzzi have sent messages. They are most ashamed that the attack occurred in their home, and anxious to have you forgive them for their neglect."

"It was not their fault," she answered. "Please do not let them distress themselves."

His mouth set, his voice was harsh. "They should not have allowed you to leave without me. I was very angry."

"No, no, it was my fault. I knew something was wrong. I insisted on leaving—" Tears came to her eyes, and her voice faltered. At once he bent over her, caressing her cheek gently.

"Do not be upset, dearest. Calm yourself. I am not angry with you. Later I will explain what occurred, and you will have more care of yourself in the future."

"Who was it? Those men—why did they—"

"All in good time," he replied, and would say no more.

For the next three days she rested, slept, and ate obediently the soft foods they gave her. And finally she was over the fever, her shoulder was healing. She lay on a lounge on the balcony, enjoying the warmth of morning sunlight on her hands and face.

Carmela had dressed her in a white nightgown of frothy lace, with a matching dressing gown which fastened to her throat and fell in lace over her hands. The violet ribbons were the only spot of color. Her hair had been brushed out and fastened back informally with a violet ribbon. Giorgio came to see her in midmorning.

"So—you are much better, and looking like a good child," he teased her. She frowned at him.

"I am not a child," she said with cool dignity. "I am quite grown up, and married. I beg you to remember that!" The flash of anger surprised him, and he sat down beside her, warily watching her face.

"So you are," he said, and changed the subject. "Your father has my permission to come this afternoon. Will you be strong enough to receive him?"

"Oh, yes, yes," she said, diverted as he had meant for her to be. "I am anxious to see Papa. Will my sisters accompany him today?"

"Not today," he said firmly. "They must await until you are stronger. I will not have you wearied by too many visitors."

She hesitated, then reached out to take his hand, so near hers. "Giorgio—tell me now," she said.

"What shall I tell you?" he asked, his fingers closing convulsively about hers, then easing.

"About those men," she said softly. "Who were they? Why did they attack me?"

"Ah—yes." He watched her face carefully as he told her, as though anxious not to have her distressed. "The story began a long time ago, so long I will not weary you with the beginnings of it. Sufficient to say, there is a family by the name of Doria, from Pisa. An ancestor of mine found one of the Dorias offensive and bullying—my great-great-grandfather, many years ago. He killed the man. His people came looking for revenge, there was a battle, and the Dorias must retreat to Pisa. Since then, they will come over to Florence, and enter any battle against us."

"And they came in the late wars," she murmured.

"Yes, they did. The head of the family now is a wolf named Enrico Doria. There is also a younger brother named Marco. But worst is Taddeo Doria, a tough and brutal killer who cares not what he does if it will bring harm to others."

"Giorgio—" She hesitated, then plunged ahead recklessly. "Were the Doria the ones who captured you—your family—who tortured you?"

His hands closed on hers again, and his eyes blazed. "Yes, they were the ones. I do not know how they heard of my mission. But at the gates of Florence they surrounded me, and carried me off. Not content with that, they—" His voice stopped, as though he were choking. He bent his head.

"I understand, Giorgio. Do not torment yourself. I should not have asked. But I want to know about all that hurts and harms you. I am—so sorry." She could not help recalling that it was her father who had betrayed him. How could he have done it? It must have been accidental, something to do with his mission. . . .

"Poor child. It was over and done long ago, there is no need for you to have been dragged into this," Giorgio said wearily. He drew his hands from hers, and stood up to pace back and forth on her small balcony, gazing out over the lush, green gardens below, at the tall, black cypresses which lined the hedges, at the flower plots of scarlet and yellow. Presently he excused himself, and went down to his study to work, leaving her with bitter thoughts. Could he forgive her for belonging to the family that had betrayed him to the Doria?

Was it this which stood between them as surely as one of the massive stone walls that surrounded the fields outside Florence? Or was it the woman she had heard spoken of at the concert, that Maria Luisa? If he had loved Maria Luisa, surely she could have soothed the harsh bitterness from him, and married him years ago.

No, he had not married Maria Luisa, he had married Viola. She drew a deep sigh, and Carmela came out quietly.

"You must come in and sleep for a time, Miss Viola," she said anxiously. "Your father comes this afternoon. You must be bright and charming for him, eh?"

She allowed herself to be persuaded to rest, but she could not sleep for thinking of the tangle they were all in.

Giorgio came up to her at luncheon, and trays were brought for them both. She cheered up a bit, for it was the first time they had eaten together since her illness. They laughed a little and chatted eagerly together. She sat up in a chair, and Giorgio would lean over to beg her to try another mouthful of the boiled fish, and some of the fresh peas.

"I am not a baby, to be fed!" she protested.

"Are you not?" he asked. "Open your mouth–" And deftly he put another spoonful of custard inside. He laughed at her grimace of annoyance, and she was happy at least that she could make him laugh, though she did not care at all for his attitude toward her.

He ate well himself, and drank some of the red wine that Carmela had brought up. He seemed much more cheerful than he had that morning, as though he had resolved to put his sad thoughts behind him.

The trays were carried away practically empty, and Carmela beamed approvingly at them both. "So–you both improve in health," she said smartly. "The good *Signore* eats little when his wife is ill. Now you are both in good health, eh?"

Viola giggled at the look he gave her, of resigned frustration. When Carmela had left them, he leaned over and kissed her forehead.

"How good to hear your laughter again, *mia cara*," he said. "*Per Dio*, when I saw you that night, and thought I might never see those lovely eyes open again–" He shuddered. "You were still as death, and the blood on your dress–God, may I never live through such a moment again."

She put out her hand to the face so near hers, and dared to stroke his cheek. He turned his face, and pressed his lips to her palm, then held it against his rough cheek.

"You are so young, so smooth–like silk," he murmured. When Carmela returned and entered without knocking, Viola could have cried aloud in rage. They had been so close for just a moment.

"Your father arrives," said Carmela happily. "You wish to change to a dress, Miss Viola?"

Giorgio said sternly, "No, she is not to move. And he is not to weary you, *cara*."

He stood up as Sir Anthony Marchmont was shown into Viola's drawing room. But the diplomat, usually so correct, ignored his host and went directly to Viola. He bent over her, anxiously studied her face, and kissed her cheek.

"My dearest little one, how are you?"

"I am recovering very well, Father. How good of you to come!"

"I would have come at once, but Giorgio and the doctor forbade it." He then turned to Giorgio, and held out his hand. The two men shook hands, and Viola watched them soberly. Did she misunderstand, or did they seem closer and more open with each other? "She looks as though she has been most ill. You are sure the doctor knows what he is doing?"

The blurted words did not anger Giorgio; he looked at Sir Anthony quite kindly, and nodded. "He is the best in Florence, probably in Tuscany. I have known him for many years. He is skillful, even brilliant in his practice of medicine."

"Good, good." Sir Anthony accepted a chair next to Viola and bent toward her again. "Your sisters send their most loving regards, and a multitude of flowers. I left them below. They are anxious to see you for themselves, but I assured them I would report most accurately. How do you feel, my little one?"

She assured him again that she felt well, and he patted her hand. "Good, good, and now Giorgio must tell me everything that happened. I do not understand."

Viola looked at her husband. She did not understand either.

Giorgio seated himself near the end of her lounge, where he could watch her face for signs of tiring. "We had set out for the palace of Count Peruzzi for a concert. Six of my men were with us. I received a note, which I later discovered to be a ruse, delivered by a man I trusted. It asked my advice concerning certain dyes to be used in a new fabric, and it was so garbled that I was upset, and left Viola to go on alone to the concert. Dolt that I was! To be drawn by such a game! I arrived at the factory to learn that no one there had sent for me. At once I knew, and hastened to return."

He paused to draw a deep breath.

"We were set upon on the lower road," he said calmly. "We fought them off, the three of us. The man with the note had told me that the note was given him by one he knew only slightly. I decided to trust him, but took him back with us. On the lower road, he was attacked with the rest of us, and received a dagger thrust to his throat. We stayed with the man until he died, an hour later. We had beaten off the attack, however. Viola, is this too much for your listening?" he asked, suddenly bending toward her.

It was almost unendurable, learning of his danger. But she wanted to hear the whole story. She forced herself to say, "Please continue, Giorgio. I would learn it all."

Her father took her hand comfortingly, and squeezed it. She felt even more reassured that he should be so concerned for her, and was warmed by his evident trust of Giorgio.

"But this is incredible! In this day and age, and in

the daylight when anyone might see you! How did they dare? Did you recognize any of them?"

"I knew two of them, though I had not seen them for years. Dogs that ran with the pack of Doria. I was anxious to reach Viola, yet even then I did not suspect that they meant to attack her. I thought their daggers were pointed only at me. Then I heard the sounds of struggle, the shouting at the Peruzzi palace. We raced on to find Viola wounded, and Benito unconscious. Count Peruzzi and others had dashed down the steps, and were vigorously routing them when we arrived. The men ran off in the darkness, and it was unsafe to try to follow. Cowards though they are, they might have attacked again from the safety of the night and the trees."

"God, it is horrible," muttered Sir Anthony, paling at the story. "So my little Viola has been drawn into this! My dearest, you must find it in your heart to forgive us both for forcing you into this tangle. It should have remained between Giorgio and me to resolve our difficulties." The apology had been hard for him to say, and he was much distressed.

Giorgio was looking directly at her. Viola said courageously, "Father, I married Giorgio of my own will, admiring and respecting him for his courage and his honor. I regret nothing. Now, let us speak no more of forgiveness. I am—happy in my new home."

Her father kissed her cheek, and Giorgio gazed at her intently. She felt flushed and as warm as with a fever, but she had had to say the words.

Sir Anthony changed the subject with his accustomed skill. "You are happy in your home," he said ruefully, "but ours goes ill. Eleanor will have told you of the servants leaving, for no one can speak Italian to them. Giorgio was right when he said we would miss you the most. Nothing goes well any longer! The girls fuss constantly, and talk of nothing but returning to London. However, I cannot accompany them now, and they dislike the chaperone I have chosen for them. How hard is my life now!" He smiled charmingly, and made a despairing gesture with a graceful hand.

"Oh, I do hope they will not give up and return to London so soon," said Viola with more politeness than genuine regret. "Do encourage Eleanor to learn Italian, she is so smart she will soon know it well."

"I will tell her you said so, but she has set her mind stubbornly against it. Ah, you are like your mother. I did not realize how much until you had left. You have always smoothed out the differences between us all, and kept us content!"

The butler came in with a tray of brandy and a glass of lime juice for Viola. She sipped slowly, enjoying the conversation between her husband and her father. Inevitably they began to speak of the war years.

"You recall the spy named Henri? I met him again in London. He was of the old aristocracy, but when the Bonaparte were thrown out and the Bourbons restored, his lands still were withheld. He was very bitter, and ready to offer his services to any who would buy them."

"I am sorry to hear it," said Giorgio. "He was not a bad fellow. What did you advise him?"

Sir Anthony answered gravely, and at length. He had advised Henri to begin again in a new country, and had given him money to sail to America. He had received a letter from him stating that the man was happier there, that he was working as a printer and would repay the sum eventually. The conversation then turned to the fates of others they had known in the war.

He did not remain long, but excused himself when Viola leaned her head back wearily and closed her eyes. "But you are tired, my dear. All this talk of war—we should have known better. I shall leave now, we have a reception to attend this evening. May I give your assurance to your sisters that you are much improved?"

She told him to do so, and he kissed her again before he left.

Carmela brought up some of her sisters' flowers in vases and bowls, and they filled the drawing room with the fragrance of roses and camellias. She was grateful for her sisters' concern, but her thoughts soon returned to Giorgio, and the puzzle of their relationship.

CHAPTER 11

Viola began to improve more rapidly, and soon was impatient to be up and about her duties. But the doctor forbade it, and Giorgio too was strict with her. They permitted her to be dressed in the morning, though, and to lie on her lounge in the drawing room of her suite.

One afternoon she was dressed in her violet muslin, with a violet ribbon threaded through her hair, when Giorgio came up after luncheon. He looked rather cross.

"Viola, the Count and Countess Peruzzi have come, and insist on seeing you. It is their third trip in as many days, and I finally promised to ask if you were strong enough to receive them for a few minutes."

He seemed quite displeased at their insistence. But Viola sat up eagerly against her little pile of violet and blue cushions, and said, "Oh, but I do wish to receive them! Please, Giorgio, allow them to come. I should dearly love to make better acquaintance with the Countess Lucia. She is a dear person."

His face relaxed, and he disappeared, to return almost immediately with the handsome couple. Countess Lucia bent to kiss Viola's cheek, graceful in her pale blue muslin and matching pelisse in the latest slim silhouette from Paris. Her small bonnet was set back from her lively face.

"*Cara* Viola, you are at last improving in health! How glad we all are! You feel much better today, yes?"

Viola pressed her slim, smooth hand, and smiled up gladly at her. She had been wanting to talk to Lucia Peruzzi, for she had a feeling that the lady could provide information she wished to know. And Giorgio seemed most fond of them both.

"So much better, I thank you. Everyone has been most gracious in their inquiries."

The Count came to kiss her hand then, and began a long speech of apology; he dwelt on his shame that his villa had not been better protected, how he blamed himself for the whole matter. Viola listened for a little time, then gently interrupted him.

"If you please, sir, do not go on! It was not your fault at all. It was my impulsiveness, my anxiety to learn what had happened to Giorgio."

"And my enemies," added Giorgio grimly. "No, no, Alessandro, do not blame yourself."

Carmela came in with a bowl of flowers and stood waiting to be noticed. Lucia Peruzzi turned gracefully to her and took the bowl.

"The Count and I have long wished to make an appropriate gift to you on your wedding. I long puzzled what to give, but Giorgio kindly informed me of your tastes and likes. I hoped that this little bowl might give you pleasure, *cara* Viola." And smilingly she set the bowl on the small lacquer table beside Viola's chaise. Viola sat up eagerly to examine it.

The bowl was of fine Italian porcelain, in shades of palest blue, mauve, violet, and cream. Within it was arranged a huge bouquet of Parma violets made of precious jade leaves and amethyst flowers, with green marble stems. Viola touched one flower petal gently; it swayed on its stem. She drew a deep breath.

"Oh, how beautiful! How kind you are! I shall cherish it always, not only for its loveliness, but for your thoughtfulness." Her impulsive words brought a smile to their faces. Even the Count relaxed a little.

Viola realized that his honor had been impugned; he would never forgive himself, that a friend had been injured in his home, the wife of a dear comrade who had been entrusted to his care. Italians were deeply concerned with such matters of honor.

"We shall not remain long," began Lucia graciously, as she seated herself on a chair beside Viola. "I was warned by Giorgio that we should not soon be welcome again if we tired you!" She gave him a rueful look.

"Oh, but I have been longing for guests. I should adore to talk to you! I have much to learn about Giorgio's circle of friends, and I'm sure you could tell me how one goes on here."

"In that event, may I remove the Count and myself to my study, to discuss subjects more to our taste?" asked Giorgio, with some humor.

This suited Viola perfectly, and after her husband and the Count had left the room, she settled back into the cushions, trying to think how to approach the subject dear to her heart. But Lucia was uncommonly perceptive.

They spoke a few minutes about the smartness of

Lucia's gown, her dressmaker and the fashion gazettes she received from Paris. She promised to bring some on her next visit.

"We have known Giorgio for many years," she said then, watching Viola's face. "My husband and yours were friends from childhood, and of course all Florence knows of the Michieli family."

Viola turned to her eagerly, her face alight. "Oh, that is just what I wanted to talk to you about," she said. She blushed. "It is strange, perhaps, to you, but I did not know Giorgio long before we were married, though Papa knew him—"

"But of course it is not strange," said Lucia graciously, although, accustomed as she was to marriages among families who had known each other literally for centuries, she did find such a marriage odd. "However, I thought that as a friend of Giorgio, I might tell you little things concerning his family, his life, that you might not know. One's friends are not always so modest about a man's achievements and his family history as the man himself, especially a man like Giorgio."

Viola abandoned all thought of deception, and beamed at her new friend. "This is exactly what I wished you to tell me!" she said happily. "Please tell me everything you can remember!"

Lucia patted Viola's hand with her slim, cool one, the diamond and emerald ring flashing in the sunlight. "It is my pleasure," she said simply. "I knew we would be friends as soon as we met. That is always the way, is it not? From the first moment, one knows if the sympathy is there, the close feeling."

Viola eagerly agreed, and listened closely as the Countess began to talk seriously.

She told Viola of how the Michieli family had built

the villa four centuries ago. She spoke of the origins of the family, the *condottiere,* Andrea de Milano, who had come to Florence to offer his services to some merchants who sought to retain their power against the forces of the Pope. He had married the daughter of a wealthy silk merchant, and had finally settled down to work with his sons in the silk trade, protecting the wagon train of silk goods as it wound up into France, to the fashion capital of Paris, and even into England. Viola listened wide-eyed to these stories of long ago.

The granddaughter of the *condottiere* had married into a fine family of impoverished noblemen, who owned a small *signoria* near Florence. The man had decided to throw in his lot with the merchants, rather than fight against them to enlarge his lands.

"And so the Michieli family was begun as we know it today," ended Lucia happily, spreading out her hands eloquently. "Giorgio is the product of a noble family, a fierce *condottiere,* a silk merchant, with all the elements in him. He is an artist, a gentleman, a shrewd businessman, a fighter of honor and nobility. As you know him."

"Yes, yes, he is," murmured Viola. She lay thinking of the long line to which she had joined herself. "But Lucia, I am puzzled. Why, if he is the last of his family, did he not marry long ago. He is twenty-eight. I thought marriages in Italy were often arranged when children were young." She knew she was blushing, but she was determined to pursue the subject.

Lucia was not at all embarrassed. She glowed at relating the family history, reveled in the romance of young Viola and the older, embittered Giorgio. "No marriage had been arranged for him when the war began in Italy, *cara.* Oh, one family or another was spoken about, and some made approaches to Giorgio's father. However, Giorgio put aside all work, all personal considerations, to devote himself to the freedom of Florence. He fought bravely and well, as you probably have heard from your father. Then—" Her face shadowed, and she hesitated.

"The Doria family—his torture and—and the scars," murmured Viola anxiously. She was so afraid that Giorgio would return too soon and interrupt this longed-for discussion.

"Yes, and Giorgio was bitterly injured. He lay in hiding for weeks, months, after he escaped. Fortunately, his wounds were attended by a skillful doctor—he is the one who came to you, *cara*. But when the wars were over and he returned, how deep the scars went! Yes, we all saw the change in him, and how my husband and I mourned over it. He was hard where he had been gentle, cynical where he had been hopeful, guarded where he had been open. He had adored his family. To know they had died because of him—ah, the wound went deep. He turned from us all, and came only infrequently to our home." She drew a great sigh.

"But—but later, when he was better—" Viola prompted.

"He took up his work, yes, and went out sometimes. He was seen with this lady and that, but never was he serious. There are several ladies who hoped for much, but—" Lucia shrugged her shoulders in a typical Italian gesture, palms upraised.

"Was—was there no particular lady he favored?" Viola could not look at her, but looked instead at her shaking hands clasped in her lap.

"Oh, one or two. There was one he liked for a time, but he found out she was nothing but a pretty fool!

One Maria Luisa Bertelli, of a good family, and quite beautiful—you may have met her, of course. But Giorgio confided to Alessandro—I tell you in confidence, *cara,* for my husband is ashamed of my gossiping, but you are, after all, Giorgio's wife! Maria Luisa was told by her family to marry to improve their fortunes, and she thought Giorgio would accept her because she was pretty, and he was not! How Giorgio sneered when he related this to Alessandro! But it hurt, I know it did, for he is sensitive about his scars."

"He—he did not love her, then?"

"I cannot believe so," said Lucia thoughtfully. "One so intelligent as Giorgio, who has known a loving family, would not love such a one as her, with little heart, and a cold nature. I think he wished for a son, yet—yet he made no move to marry, not until a pretty little English girl with violets in her hands came to speak to him! No wonder he loves violets now!" And she smiled happily at Viola.

Viola heard voices approaching her room. She put out her hand quickly to Lucia's. "You will not tell them I asked—" she whispered. "I do so long to know more about him, and some subjects I *cannot* ask him—"

Lucia's eyes sparkled happily. "It is our secret, *cara,*" she said comfortably. "And I shall come again soon and tell you more, much more! But there, the men arrive!"

She turned her bewitching face to the door as they entered.

"So soon?" she mocked. "We have not yet begun to talk, and you are finished already?"

"Viola must be weary," said Giorgio, looking anxiously at her. But she lay back and smiled up at him, her eyes sparkling. "Ah, you do not look too tired," he concluded.

"Good, then I may come again soon!" Lucia arose, sweeping her skirts about her. She bent again to kiss Viola's cheek, and whispered, "And to tell you more, much more, about your so modest husband!"

"Thank you—more than I can say." And Viola squeezed her hand gratefully. "You are most gracious to bring such a beautiful gift," she said, but her eyes were eloquent with meaning.

"Next time I shall bring the fashion gazettes, though with a husband so wise in the silk trade you will be years ahead of me with no effort. Alessandro, I must have some of that new mauve silk which Giorgio is making!"

And so teasing her husband, she swept from the room, turning to blow a kiss to Viola, and giving her a slight wink from her lustrous eyes.

Giorgio escorted them to the door, and Carmela came to help Viola undress, and slip between the sheets for a good long rest. She was almost asleep when Giorgio came in softly, so he did not linger. She slept till teatime, and rose much refreshed.

Giorgio came to take tea with her. And it was then, as silently they looked out over the garden, that Viola realized that despite all her revelations, Lucia had said nothing of the Doria.

His enemies might strike again. They had not succeeded in killing her, or Giorgio. And they were the only Michieli left. If Giorgio died without a son, their revenge would be complete.

She finished her tea and lay back. "Weary?" he asked at once. "I knew she was staying too long," he added worriedly.

"No, no, I enjoyed her visit so much. I think we

shall become very good friends. She is so kind and intelligent."

Giorgio's face relaxed; he nodded approvingly. "They are good friends of mine, and I respect them. It pleases me that you will be as close to Lucia as I am to Alessandro."

"Giorgio—would you tell me something?"

He glanced at her, and his face seemed to close up cautiously. "If possible, *cara*. What is it?"

"Those—Doria. Did they return to Pisa?"

Frowning, he did not answer for a moment. "Did Lucia speak of those wolves?" he asked, his voice harsh and abrupt. "If so—"

"No, she said nothing of them."

He bit his lip. "Well—they are still about," he said. "But you are not to concern yourself about them. I have doubled the guard. Soon they will grow weary away from their families and homes, and return to Pisa. There is nothing for them here. All Florence knows them, and they are not welcome."

"But they—they could strike again—at you," and her voice trembled.

"*Cara*, do not worry about it," he said patiently, but with a hard note in his tone. "You will not be touched, I shall guard you closely. Carmela stays near always, and Benito will be your personal guard. He adores you, and will protect you with his life."

"I am thinking of you," she said flatly. "You go often to Florence—"

"With half a dozen men as escort! No, no, they will not bother us. It is not a problem. A vendetta is alive only in Sicily, I think. We Tuscans are too practical to spend our lives on such a foolish venture. And the Doria have their own work to do, they must go home and tend to their farms. No, they will not waste their time in Florence."

She was not satisfied, but his eyes flashed and his voice was unusually harsh, so she leaned back and changed the subject to the gift that Lucia had brought her.

"Is it not charming? I shall always cherish it."

"Yes, quite pretty," he said moodily. She wished she had not brought up the subject of the Doria; he was quite cross. She thought he had been trying to reassure her, when he himself was not entirely convinced that they were safe.

Or—or did he not care whether he lived or died? She thought of what Lucia had said, how bitter he was, how he had not married because of his cynicism. He had wanted a son—but what if he no longer cared enough even to have a son?

Lucia thought he had married Viola for love. But it had been for revenge, which had turned to dust in his hands. He had not been able to force himself to hurt a gentle girl in his control, and even his hatred of Sir Anthony had been dispelled. They were able to respect each other, and talk of the war years almost dispassionately. Perhaps he now understood that Sir Anthony had been guilty of carelessness, not of deliberate, malicious betrayal.

If so, then his motive for marriage was gone, and he was tied for life to a young girl he did not love. What good could come of this marriage? Did he hate the ties that bound them together? Did he long for freedom, to do as he wished?

Yet—Lucia had said that Giorgio wished for a son. He had finally married Viola; he was a married man in the eyes of the Church and his friends. Would he keep grimly to the marriage—until his death?

Did he long for death, because life was no longer sweet to him? Would he find it more sweet, and more worth living, should he have a son?

She gazed out at the garden after Giorgio left her to work for a time in his study. She scarcely saw the flaming beds of gladioli, the rose bushes, the slim columbine of red and blue and mauve, the neatly clipped green hedges. The fountain and the laughing boy clutching his dolphin friend played on, spraying fine jets of water into the air, as the garden turned dusky with late afternoon. From somewhere near the kitchens, a baritone voice was singing huskily some Italian song of love and longing.

Tears came to her eyes and were resolutely blinked away. Giorgio did not love her, but he was a man, and an Italian, with a deeply ingrained love of family. He found life bitter, work all-absorbing, because he had no family left except a young English girl whom he considered a child. A child he must take care of, protect, guard—a nuisance.

But what if Viola had a son, his son? What if he found some desire for her, and came to her at least often enough to give him a son?

"And I am not a child, I am a married woman," Viola muttered fiercely to a bird that perched on her balcony stone railing. Alarmed, the bird fled, with a dart of crimson wings against the dusky blue-mauve of the sky.

It would take daring, arts she had not learned. Still, she had watched from her corner of the family drawing room as her sisters practiced their feminine wiles on men. How had Bernice acted when she wished to draw a man to her? The lashes fluttering, the little hand gesturing gracefully soft and murmuring. And Eleanor, even dignified Eleanor, had a charm and grace of movement, her eyes eloquent as she gazed up into a man's eyes.

"I shall do it," said Viola aloud, scowling with determination. She would be embarrassed often, and perhaps Giorgio might think she had gone mad! But somehow she would find a way to encourage him to desire her. She loved him, she adored him, surely that would make up for his lack of love for her.

One day, when she could give him a child, Giorgio might find sweetness in life once more, the surge of elemental feeling for the continuation of his family, of himself into the future.

She lay thinking, and the dusk covered her hot blushes as she thought of what it would involve. She would feel like a shameless female, but surely he would understand that she wished him to desire her. There must be ways to make a man comprehend that!

And with a son, Giorgio would once again care for life. He would have someone to live for, besides a shy English girl he considered a child.

CHAPTER 12

Several days later, Viola persuaded Carmela to allow her to go downstairs to the drawing room, to surprise Giorgio when he returned home from Florence. The maid was dubious, but found her mistress quite firm. So Carmela and Benito watched carefully as she descended, hovering in case she felt faint.

Triumphantly she arrived at the blue sofa in the drawing room, and was glad to sink into the cushions. Carmela brought a rug to cover her feet, although the July day was warm. Viola sank into the cushions thankfully, and waited for Giorgio to return.

He came at his usual time, striding into the hallway. His deep crisp voice inquired of the butler, "How does the *Signora*? She is awake now?"

"*Si, signore.* She is downstairs, in the drawing room," replied the butler, and in a moment Giorgio came in, frowning at her.

"What is this? Does the doctor permit this?"

She smiled up at him daringly, her cheeks flushed,

her gray eyes shining. As he came to her and bent over her anxiously, she shyly lifted her arms. He hesitated, then bent and kissed her cheek. She closed her arms about his neck, and he sat down beside her, gazing questioningly at her.

She did not dare meet his gaze, she felt so embarrassed. But she had determined on her course. "I am practically well, Giorgio. My arm did not hurt all day."

"Good, that is good." He bent again, and kissed her cheek, his lips lingering as though he enjoyed the soft, silken texture, the feminine warmth of her.

She let her arms slide down, but one hand caressed his scarred cheek. "You are tired? Was it a difficult day, Giorgio?"

"It was as usual," he said. He took her hand and held it against his cheek tenderly, then kissed the palm. He said absently, "Your friend the countess came to see the mauve silk. She is much excited by it, and says it will be the fashionable color of this winter. We shall see."

"She has excellent taste, I believe."

"She said the same of you," he said with a half-smile. His dark eyes were grave as he studied her. "You have more color in your cheeks, I think you do improve now."

"Oh, I am well again."

"You must be careful."

Giorgio insisted on carrying her back to bed then, to her disappointment, for she had hoped to remain up longer. Still, he had not rejected her. The next day, she again waited for him. This time he came right to her, and sat down beside her, and bent to kiss her cheek. She held her arms about his neck, and her face was welcoming, though she felt like a brazen female.

Each day she forced herself to overcome her shyness, and show how glad she was to have him beside her. She asked about his work, and about their friends in Florence. He lingered beside her longer, studying her face as they talked, as though he questioned what her feelings were.

Finally the doctor took off the bandage, examined the wound critically, and determined she might leave off the bandages as long as she was careful. The wound was healing nicely, he said, though there would be a scar, reddish and puckered, all her life.

She rushed into speech. "Just so it is an honorable scar, like my husband's," she said to the doctor, intensely aware of Giorgio standing in the dimness of the room behind him.

The doctor patted her cheek in a kindly fashion. "I can say with truth that it is. But what a pity for a beautiful woman to have any scar. For a man it is different." He rose, and packed up his doctor's bag, smiling at her with a twinkle in his dark eyes that told her he knew what she was about. She did not mind at all.

After he had left, Viola drew back the edge of her violet robe and bent her head to examine the long scar. "Does it make me ugly, Giorgio?" she asked, in a deliberately provocative tone.

"Nothing could do that, *cara*," he said with quiet intensity. He came to sit on the chaise beside her, in the sunlight from the open windows of her room. Gently he touched the scar with his long fingers. "If only I could have taken this wound for you! I blame myself that I was not there."

"Oh—pooh! I should have been terribly upset if you

had been hurt, Giorgio," she said slowly, her fingers curling about his as he held her hand. "Do you know, I think it hurts one more when—when a person one loves is hurt, than when one receives a hurt—is that not true?"

He looked deeply into her gray eyes. She met the gaze, unafraid. There was a dark flush on his cheekbones.

"I am not sure I know what you mean, Viola," he said.

She held his hand more tightly in case he tried to draw it away. "I mean—when your father and mother and sister were—were hurt, and you could not help them—did it not hurt you more than anything they could do to you?"

He was silent; his eyes shut tight, and she was suddenly afraid that she had gone too far. Then he bent, and with a sigh gently rested his cheek against her scarred shoulder, "Yes, *cara,* it is true. How do you, so young and innocent of life, know this?"

She raised her hand, and very timidly stroked his thick, curly hair, loving the way it sprang under her fingers. They were silent, in the warmth and quiet of the room, alone for a time, close as never before. Then he left her to rest, but she could not sleep, her heart was so light and hopeful.

The Countess Lucia Peruzzi called again the next afternoon, and remained for tea. The two of them were deep in conversation, and when she had left, Viola felt suddenly quite weary, and fell asleep on the chaise.

Giorgio had come up several times to see her, Carmela told her when she finally wakened about eight. He had been much concerned. "And he growled about like a bear, that you might have become too weary," said Carmela, beaming down at her charge. "How he adores you, my little Viola! Yes, he does, for anything that happens to you touches him deeply. Now, you will wear the lilac silk which he likes so much."

She was bathed and dressed, and lying on the chaise again when Giorgio came up. "Ah, you look tired," he said anxiously. "That woman—I shall forbid her to come again for a month!"

"No, no, Giorgio," she coaxed, catching hold of his hand and resting it against her cheek. "I love talking to her. And I am stronger every day, you know that I am."

"You will have a light dinner on your tray—"

She pouted, and fluttered her dark eyelashes at him as Bernice did when she wished to charm a man. "But Giorgio, you said I might have dinner with you this evening! I wish to come downstairs!"

He frowned, and shook his head. "Not tonight, *cara*."

"Then have dinner with me up here!"

He finally agreed to it, and they ate at a small table set between the opened French windows. Together they watched the sun setting in a splash of orange and gold. Then dusk stole over the green gardens, turning everything to purple.

"It is so beautiful here, no wonder you love it," she breathed, turning to him, her eyes glowing. She sipped again at the champagne he had ordered for them; she felt light-headed and rather reckless. The way he gazed at her with his dark eyes, looking from her hair to her face, to her shoulders and the low neck of her gown, to her white arms, to her small waist—it all made her a little dizzy.

Giorgio drank down the rest of his champagne, and

refilled his glass. "The setting is for you as pure gold for a rare gem," he said in a low tone.

The footman and Carmela removed the trays, and Viola lay down again on the chaise. They had left the champagne. Giorgio filled her glass and brought it to her again.

He sat down beside her as she sipped, and peeped at him over the brim of the glass. He did seem to like being near her. Did he feel anything for her beside compassion? If only he felt desire, it might be enough. She felt as though she had enough love welling up in her for them both.

She finished the wine, and set the glass on the low table beside her. Giorgio set his own glass beside it, and deliberately bent over her. His cheeks were flushed, there in the dimness of the drawing room, relieved only by the last light from the sky and a few candles over the mantel.

"Viola," he said huskily. "You are so beautiful, so dear. Let me—touch you—like this, as one touches a rare piece of ivory, a lovely statuette."

His mouth touched her cheek lightly. She raised her arms and linked them behind his neck. "But I am not a statue," she breathed against his cheek. "I am—a woman. Am I not? Don't you know I am warm—and alive—" Her head turned as she spoke, and he must have turned his at the same moment, for their lips touched, clung, hesitated, then he crushed his mouth down hungrily on hers.

Her breath caught, and she clung to him as he pressed kiss after kiss on her mouth. She opened her mouth to speak, and he stilled the words with his opened lips moving on hers, so that breath became sighs, and one caress blended into the next. He had slipped one arm under her, holding her to him closely, and the other hand was moving slowly from her shoulder down her bare arm, to the silken cloth over her rounded breasts. At his touch, she seemed to turn to fire, to molten lava; her bones melted to wax in his clasp.

He did not seem to be able to hold her close enough. His head moved, so that his face was against her bare throat, and warm kisses moved from her chin to the hollow between her breasts. His hand had moved down to her waist, lingered, caressed, then slid to her hips, his fingers deft in rousing her to lovely madness.

She could not think, she could only feel. Giorgio was kissing her at last, was holding her as she had hungered to be held. His lips were learning her soft flesh. His free hand went to her breasts, and deliberately he unfastened the tiny buttons, one by one down to her waist. He drew aside the fabric, and kissed her on the curves of her breasts. She could scarcely breathe; her mouth was open, and sighs came storming from her at the sweetness of his touch, the wild sensations he roused in her.

He was murmuring in Italian, and how glad she was that she knew what he said. "My darling, my adored, how beautiful you are, how you melt into my arms. Your lips are heady as wine. I die of longing for you—" He came back to her lips, claiming them with passionate desire. She answered him, kiss for kiss, all shyness gone, wanting him as freely as he wanted her.

Presently he drew back from her a little. She murmured a protest. "Giorgio—Giorgio—kiss me again—"

"My love, I want you," he murmured. "Do you feel strong enough to take this? I cannot continue to kiss you without wanting to take you completely. Oh, my darling—"

"I love you," she whispered, her arms clinging. "Giorgio—oh, Giorgio—"

He did not hesitate any longer. He rose, then picked her up and carried her to her bedroom. The blankets and sheets had been turned back demurely, and a single candle burned beside the bed, sheltered in its glass globe.

There was enough light for him to undress her. She loved the look on his face as he drew off her dress, her silken undergarments, her little slippers, and unfastened the pins from her hair. Her blond hair slid down to her shoulders, tumbled in his fingers.

"In a minute, darling," he assured her passionately, as he finally rose from the bed. He flung off his clothes, and came to her. His face was hard with passion, his lips upturned with adoration and desire; his dark eyes glittered as the candle flickered.

He lay down beside her, and bent over her.

She had thought he would move to take her at once, and make her his wife. She had resolved not to cry out, not to spoil any moment of passion between them. But Giorgio, she found, was too skilled for this.

He adored her with his lips, with his fingers, with his arms and his whole body. His hand trailed down over her body, leaving little flames in its wake. She trembled, and her hands when he held her went urgently to his strong back, to cling to him. It seemed that everything in her longed for him to claim her completely. But still he waited.

His lips moved over hers, teasing her, drawing her into long, lingering kisses. His hand went over and over her breasts, down to her waist, to her thighs, learning her, wakening her to what it meant to know the passionate desire of a strong man. When finally he moved, and began to claim her, she was completely ready, clinging to him, holding him hungrily, anxious for him to be a part of her. In silence, they met, and held.

She knew surprise. Was this what it was about? All this closeness, this warmth, this sweetness? Little pain, that soon over, and the marvelous knowledge of each other, emotion rising to an ecstasy that made her heart quicken wildly, her mind blanking out all else in the world.

When it was over, and he drew back, she felt keen loss, and sleepily murmured her protest. He drew her into the circle of his arms, and against his hard bare chest, she slept at last.

She wakened some time in the night, and lay awake for a time, wondering, happy, amazed. It had happened, and it was so good, so marvelous. Giorgio had been a perfect lover to her, and she was grateful, relieved, and excited.

He was there when she wakened slowly in the morning. She felt first a little tugging of her loose curls, and opened her sleepy eyes to see his face close to hers. A smile curved her mouth.

"A good morning to you, my adored," he whispered.

"Oh, Giorgio, I thought I was dreaming," she said sleepily, as he kissed her cheek, her throat, her mouth.

"It is I who dream, and do not wish to rouse from it," he murmured against her throat. And it was a long time before he wanted to rise and go to his own room, to bathe and dress. "You will stay in bed, *cara,* until noon at least. I will come and kiss you before I leave."

"When will you come home?"

He laughed softly. "Will you miss me?" he teased.

"I always miss you," she told him honestly. When he had left her, she yawned and stretched, and snuggled down into the pillows again. She was almost asleep when he came in, and kissed her farewell for the day.

So the pattern of their lives changed abruptly. He came home earlier, and found her waiting for him in the drawing room, and always there was a kiss and an intimate word of loving for her. He slept with her each night and she no longer had nightmares, but wakened happily into his arms.

The hard look of Giorgio's face had softened so remarkably that others remarked on it, and were pleased. "Ah, marriage is good for you both," Lucia teased one day, when she and Viola were having tea together.

Viola laughed and blushed. She was so happy that she was almost afraid. Giorgio was a warm, passionate lover, more demanding and loving than she had ever dreamed he would be. "Isn't marriage good for every woman, especially when she has someone like—Giorgio," she said softly, her eyes dreaming.

"Not always, for not everyone *is* a Giorgio," Lucia assured her dryly. "Now, my Alessandro, he is a good soul, but sometimes he worries and frets too much, and I have to coax him into good humor. Your Giorgio thinks only of pleasing you, of designing fabrics that will suit his English rose. I had to assure him three times that the pale blue silk he had designed was not suitable for me! For he was thinking only of you."

"Oh, Lucia, you tease me so!"

Lucia patted her warm cheek, and laughed. "It is

good to be young and in love, *cara,* is it not? Does Giorgio consent to your coming to our villa for a concert next week?"

"Oh—I forgot to ask him!"

When Giorgio came home that day, he brought her violets, a small gray kitten in a basket for her to cherish and amuse, and a golden bracelet set with sapphires to match her engagement ring. All thoughts of outings flew from her head, but when she spoke of it later, he frowned and shook his head. "Not this summer, *cara.* They will come to us. I have ordered some musicians for a little party next week, if you are strong enough. But I will not have you exposed to danger."

"Oh!" She stared at him blankly. In her newfound happiness, she had forgotten the vendetta! Grayness spread over her little world, her mouth drooped. "I had forgotten—oh, Giorgio, have the Doria not left Florence?"

He put his hand under her chin, and caressed her lips with his thumb. His dark eyes glowed at her. "Forget them, my darling. They will not trouble you. No, I think only of you. The doctor warned that you might not be strong for a time, and I, careless that I am, have not been easy with you these weeks."

She blushed, and turned her cheek into his palm like the small kitten that curled into her lap. She adored being cherished like this. "I—I do not mind, Giorgio. You know that," she said in a small voice.

He bent and brushed his lips caressingly against hers. "I know. You are generous and loving in my arms, as in all that you do. Be careful a little longer, and rebuke me if I am too demanding of you."

But she would not do that. She loved his demands, and only wished she were able to match his passion with her own. She was growing in love, but sometimes she thought he must consider her still young and naïve.

His tone was ever indulgent, he showered her with gifts and thoughtfulness. But sometimes he still treated her like a child, not telling her his thoughts and worries. Would he ever consider her a real wife?

He picked her up from the chaise, and sat down in a large armchair, holding her against his strength. She rested her head against his shoulder, and was happy when he rubbed his scarred cheek against her smooth young face, and kissed her mouth. Someday he would know that she loved him completely, and wanted to be the wife he needed.

CHAPTER 13

Presently it was September, and Viola was quite well again. She and Giorgio began to visit their friends occasionally. They were welcomed in a way that warmed her shy heart. And Giorgio seemed to have changed remarkably, everyone told her.

"Now he is his old self," said Alessandro Peruzzi, as he danced with her one evening in their enchanting villa. "How we rejoice to see him smile again, and dance. Before the wars, he was always gay and laughing. He will not be completely that way again, yet we know he is happy with his so charming wife."

Viola smiled up at him. Lucia had become her closest friend, and she felt more at ease with the stern Alessandro, knowing he felt deep friendship for Giorgio. "How kind you are to say so," she murmured. "I am so happy also. Do you know—the Doria have left Florence, have they not?"

He frowned down at her, with a touch of hardness. "You are not to worry your pretty head about that!

Giorgio would be furious with me if I discussed the matter! He will protect you, do not fear."

She did fear, and always would, not for herself but for Giorgio. If anything happened to him, the light in her life would go out.

She was pleased when her sisters came to the villa twice to visit with her. It was a long journey, but they seemed delighted by her home, rather jealous to be sure, but suppressing their envy admirably, with practiced charm. Eleanor was being courted by Reginald Selby, which caused Viola some concern. She did not like the man, and felt she never could. But he was a diplomat, and she had always felt that Eleanor would marry a man of their father's profession.

Bernice was adored by every man who came near her, with her kittenish ways, and her beauty. She fell in love twice a month, Eleanor said dryly, and her father was threatening to make a match for her and be done with it. "But he would not be so cruel," said Bernice, tossing her curls.

Viola smiled and was amused by them, but more concerned over Giorgio's imminent trip to Rome. He would be gone for four days, and she did not know how she would endure his absence. She would imagine all sorts of calamities until he returned.

When her sisters heard of the journey, they said at once that Viola must come to them. She refused. "No, I will remain here. This is my home," she said decisively.

She said farewell to Giorgio that bright September day, with dread in her heart. She clung to him when he would have left, and he gave her one more kiss, and reassured her.

"It is only four days, *cara*. You will be all right. And I promise—yes, again—that I will be most careful.

Benito will guard you, and I have four men with me."

He left, and she waved the carriage out of sight, then turned back slowly into the empty room. How quiet the villa was when Giorgio was gone. Dread filled her. She paced from one room to another, and refused to eat.

Carmela scolded her. "How can a woman cling like that? A man must be about his business, you know this!"

"But Carmela, I am afraid for him," she whispered. "What if the Doria follow him? The road to Rome is long, and there are places where he might be ambushed."

"You must put all such thoughts from your head!" said Carmela sternly. "You will be ill when he returns, and what will he say to me then?"

A note came from her sisters the next day. They begged her to attend a party at the home of Reginald Selby. Sir Anthony also wished her to come. The family must become better acquainted with him, and perhaps Eleanor could then make up her mind about the man.

"Perhaps it would help to pass the time, to think of this," said Viola to her confidante, Carmela. "Should I go, do you think?"

"Yes, do go, little one. I do not care for the man myself. But a house tells much of a man; perhaps you may be able to understand him more, and be able to advise your sister."

"She would not listen to me, I think," Viola said.

"Your father might listen. He thinks much of your opinion, I notice, even more since you have so charmed the good *Signore*, your husband. Indeed, you have matured much since your marriage."

Viola finally decided to go, and sent her acceptance.

Then she debated what to wear. She finally settled on a blue silk dress with matching cloak and bonnet with white ruching, in the new, smaller shape, which sat on the back of her curls.

Benito and two men would accompany her, and it would still be early when she returned. So the next afternoon they set out, she in the carriage, Benito and the two men riding beside the carriage, one of their best drivers on the seat.

The sky was ominous that September afternoon. Dark clouds rolled up in the west and cast shadows across the road and down into Florence. She leaned toward the window and gazed out, wondering how Giorgio did in Rome. It was a long journey. Was he weary? Did he miss her?

Soon it began to rain. Little splashes of water hit her face, and others made a patter on the roof of the carriage. Oh, she wished she had not started out! It would be a miserable day, and it would not relieve her longing for Giorgio one bit.

She heard Benito call out sharply in Italian, someone replied, then she heard the sound of a shot. Her hand flew to her breast.

"What is it?" she cried out.

The driver said, "Keep inside, *ma donna!* Men have stopped us—" The carriage had pulled up when another shot rang out. The rider closest to the carriage fell from the saddle slowly, his foot caught in the stirrup.

Then another shot, and another. She reached futilely for her small handbag. She had no weapon at all, not even a knife. She had not thought of carrying one, not even the small, elegant dagger that Giorgio had given her, the mate for the one he carried.

The carriage started again, and jolted ahead. Had

her driver been able to fight them off? She heard the sound of horses trotting along, then another gunshot. Fearfully she peered out; she could not see Benito or any of the Michieli guards.

The carriage was going on at a sharp clip. She called up to the driver outside. "What is happening? What is it?"

No answer, and then fear took hold of her. The carriage was traveling rapidly, and now they had turned off on a dark road, away from Florence. They were jolting along under avenues of cypresses and oaks, and she thought they must be headed toward Prato.

A man she had never seen before passed the window, and seeing her peer out fearfully, gave her a broken, evil grin. His teeth were like fangs, she thought, shrinking back.

The ride went on and on. Rain drummed on the roof of the carriage, and it was growing darker. She thought an hour passed, then another. And another. The road was unfamiliar now. No one passed them, and the carriage was jolting over such uneven surfaces that she thought they must have left the main road.

Finally the carriage pulled up, and she saw the dim lights of a villa on a hillside. The horsemen pulled up around her. She saw now that there were half a dozen men, dark-visaged, grinning, staring frankly at her.

Someone opened the carriage, but she held back. An arm reached in and caught at her roughly, then hauled her out. "Here she is, the pretty *signora*," said the man in harsh Italian.

A man hurried down the steps, regardless of the pouring rain. She saw his face—the hard face of Reginald Selby!

She drew herself up. The unknown was known, and

could be faced with less fear. "What is the meaning of this, Mr. Selby?" she asked haughtily.

"You have come to my party, as requested, little Viola," he smiled. "Come inside. I regret that your sisters have not yet arrived. I fear they went to my town house instead of my country villa." As she tried to draw back, he caught at her arm and pulled her rudely up the broken steps of the villa.

He hustled her into the first room they came to, a dusty drawing room, little-used, she guessed. She glimpsed a few pieces of furniture of indifferent nature, a sofa covered with faded velvet, and half a dozen gilded chairs with flecks of paint peeling from them. Over the mantel was set a pair of dulled swords, and several candles were lit behind dusty glass globes.

He turned her to face him, his green eyes mocking and keen. "You were not followed?" he asked of one of his men, still studying Viola's face.

"No, *signore*. The men fought, but they were no match for us. We left them in the road."

"I told you to finish them off."

"*Si, signore*. I think they were finished." He sounded lazy, indifferent. Reginald Selby cursed him in English and in Italian, but the man only shrugged, and went to lean against the mantel, his look going over Viola in an insulting way.

"No matter. If they are found, all the better," said Selby at last, and pushed Viola rudely down on the sofa. "Sit down before you faint. We will have a wait until your good husband arrives. Two days or three, no matter. You will entertain me until he comes. It will be very amusing. The prim little girl who looked at me so coldly will be very warm to me for her husband's sake? Eh?" He flicked a finger under her soft chin, and laughed as she flinched from his touch.

A large bottle of brandy was brought to him, and two glasses. Selby poured out some of the dark liquid, and offered it to her. She shook her head. He tossed off his glass, and poured more. From the thickness of his voice and the flush on his face, she guessed he had been drinking steadily for some time.

Giorgio, oh, Giorgio, she thought, in agony. She looked down at her hands, folded primly in her lap. She was the bait, the bait for the man who had almost died years ago, who had lived to escape from his enemies.

Selby sat down in a broken-down armchair, and cursed as it sagged beneath him. He drank more brandy, then fixed his green eyes on her.

"You might as well remove your bonnet and prepare to be comfortable, little girl," he said coldly. "Your husband has enough clues to find us readily. I count on his impetuous nature to bring him racing to us, where we will finish him off. We should have done it long ago. He is in Rome, however; it will take some time for him to come."

She spoke finally, her tone as cool and composed as she could manage. "So it was you who betrayed him five years ago. Giorgio and his family."

Selby shrugged, his eyes glinting in the candlelight. As he faced her, she could see the heavy lines around his mouth, the gray streaks in his hair, the sagging of his chin from the years of dissipation.

He said nothing, but merely watched her with a glow in his eyes. As he looked her up and down, she shrank from that look as from a desecration.

"Giorgio"—it made her feel stronger to say her husband's name—"Giorgio will not know where I am."

"He will know. I left enough clues for him to follow. I let it be known I was going to my home in the country. Your sisters will be puzzled when I do not turn up for my own party in Florence."

"How can you live in Florence again after this?" she asked steadily. "All Florence will know and hate you!"

He laughed. "Why should I remain? I shall have completed the task I set myself to do!"

Then she knew. Selby had indeed betrayed Giorgio years ago. Probably for money from the French. He must have money secreted somewhere, and once he had satisfied himself by killing the one man who had escaped his net years ago, he would disappear, and make a new start somewhere else.

"And you can live with yourself, after such a betrayal?"

He cursed her, deliberately, watching the flush rising in her face as she listened to his harsh, coarse words. When he had finished, he flung his glass to the mantel, where it shattered, sending glass and brandy over the dingy white wood.

He picked up the other glass and filled it, drinking steadily until it was empty. "You will say nothing again unless I direct you, little Viola," he said at last. "You will not insult me. You will be a good little girl, and keep me warm tonight, eh? It will be delicious to see the expression on the face of the good *Signor* Michieli, the hero of Florence, when he realizes I have had you for two or three days and nights! His precious little wife! I shall treat you as I please, and my revenge will be all the sweeter!"

Her blood seemed to turn to ice within herself. To be the prey of this man, this bloody-handed villain who had caused the torture of Giorgio. . . .

With a great effort, she kept herself outwardly calm. Her hands did not move. She said, without a tremor, "So it *was* you who betrayed him? Was it also you who caused the deaths of his mother and father and sister? You betrayed his mission, and enabled the Doria to capture him?"

He cursed again, and left the room. She sagged with relief, but remained erect as long as she could. It was quite dark outside now, and the rain continued to pour down, a dull, steady sound on the roof of the small villa. It had probably been used as a hunting lodge for many centuries, she thought, looking at the heads of animals on the walls, the swords crossed over the mantel, a rusty pistol in a case in the cupboard. There were few comforts in it, no signs that a woman had been there.

Selby returned with a tray of food. She wondered if it had been drugged, and watched with seeming carelessness as he served her plate. No, he served both of them from the same bowl, so she felt she could eat, and she must keep up her strength. If he took her, it would not be without a fight!

She refused the brandy, asked politely for tea, and was cursed for her trouble. But another Italian brought a teapot to her, a cup, and some boiling water, and she made the tea with steady hands, and drank a cup of it. It gave her strength and warmth.

Selby was watching her intently, his face flushed and greedy with lust. He pushed back his plate, wiped his mouth with his napkin, and sent the Italian from the room. The man grinned down at Viola, and slouched away carelessly, leaving the door open.

"So—we are alone, little one."

"Yes, I should like to talk with you," she said steadily.

"I did not bring you here for speech!"

"Nevertheless, I should like to know some things. When my father learned of Giorgio's mission, did he tell you of it?"

Selby shrugged. "Your father betrayed him. You know that."

She thought for a time, quite calmly. No, it did not make sense anymore. Why else would Selby be so intent on killing Giorgio, if he had not been so involved years ago? Only her father's place in the puzzle bewildered her. Had he told Selby, knowing what the man would do?

It was pitch-dark outside. The rain blew gusts against the windows, lightning flashed, and thunder rolled over their heads. The candle on the table beside her gutted and went out. The candles on the mantel were low.

When it was dark in the room, would he take her? Would she die of it? Oh, Giorgio, she thought. How tender he had been. She knew this man would not be; he was lustful and cruel. Giorgio—my Giorgio, she thought, and clasped her hands tightly together. She must be strong for him, she must be calm, or Selby would turn on her like an animal, and rend her.

"You were fond of Eleanor," she said quietly then, as he drank. "Had you thought of her emotions in this?"

"I care nothing for any woman. I would not marry. She thinks only of clothes and power."

"I am sure you are wrong about that. Eleanor is a warm-hearted woman. She used clothes and charm as a weapon only in the gentle warfare of love," said Viola, feeling her palms sweating. She must keep talking, say anything to divert him.

"Ha! My experience with women tells me otherwise. She would break a whip over my head if she could! No woman gets me in her power," and Selby grinned at her, studying her from head to foot. "You have made the good *Signor* Michieli happy, yes? You must have become a woman. I shall learn how much you know tonight. Perhaps I can teach you a few new tricks, before your husband comes for you, and I end everything for you both."

So he meant to kill them both. Her heart was pounding; she was not at all sure she could keep up her show of cool indifference, her conversation with this mad beast. He must be mad, she thought. He must be insane, to care so little for anything but hate and revenge. Even Giorgio, although he said he wanted revenge, had not shown such hatred or cruelty. And all thoughts of revenge had gone from him once he had Viola in his home. He had thought only of giving her gentleness and comfort, beautiful clothes and jewels, and happiness.

The thought of Giorgio held her steady. She clung to it. Had he learned yet of her capture? He would come to her rescue, but surely he would be clever about it! He would not ride into this horrible trap.

The silence had lasted too long. Selby stood up lazily and reached for her, grabbing her arm. His fingers seemed to grip her like steel, hurting the tender flesh.

"Come on, Viola, Let's find a bed. I am sure you must want some sleep. You can have some, after I'm satisfied!"

He yanked her up. Then they both heard the sound of hooves. He let her go abruptly, and shoved her down on the sofa.

"It cannot be him—not so soon." He muttered to himself, and went to the door, shouting for his men.

"We have him! We have him!" one of the Italians called back. Viola sprang up, her hands clasped, her face agonized.

"Giorgio—" She watched the door as the men came up the steps from the road below. Selby watched, too, lounging against the doorframe, his hand on his dagger. Then he went alert.

"Damn it all!" he muttered. He stood back to allow the men to enter. The first man was older, mud-stained, his face anxious, his graying hair wet and mussed from the wind and rain. He went straight to Viola.

"Papa!" she cried, and went into his arms. She felt them close about her spasmodically, holding her to his wet cloak.

He whispered in her ear, urgently, "He has not harmed you?"

"Not yet," she said faintly. "But he said—tonight—he would rape— He has set a trap for Giorgio, but he means to kill us both!"

She felt the shudder that went through her father. Sir Anthony held her tightly for a moment, then pushed her down gently on the sofa, and turned to Selby.

"I must ask you now to allow me to take my daughter home," he said with quiet dignity.

Selby scowled at him. "Damn you, you would come, would you? Well, no matter. You may join her in waiting!"

He turned on them both, and slammed from the room.

CHAPTER 14

A dark Italian with unshaven face and slanted dark eyes leaned against the doorframe near the veranda. He seemed to ignore the two seated on the sofa, yet Viola knew he was aware of every move they made.

She and her father sat silently for a time, hands clasped. He looked older than she had ever seen him, grayed, fatigued, his shoulders slumping. Oddly, she had never loved him so much. He had come to her, risking the danger to himself.

She pressed his hand at last. "How did you know?" she murmured.

He stirred, sighed. "I accompanied your sisters to Selby's home. I was uneasy about Eleanor's interest in him. I had come to suspect, to guess—you see, years ago, when Giorgio's mission was planned, Selby was my aide. I trusted him. I was terribly busy, and left many details to him. I told him of the mission. Yes, it was my foolishness. Now I realize I was merely his tool. He came out of the wars too well. He had money to burn—he spent much, yet always had more. The French must have paid him well for his information—which he learned right in my office, from my very lips!"

"He hates Giorgio," said Viola flatly. "Do you know why?"

"He always disliked Giorgio and tried to undermine my confidence in him. Yet I trusted Giorgio; he was a man of honor in everything he did. He went on missions alone, refusing to draw anyone else with him into danger. His courage, his daring, his imagination, led him to succeed in the most hairbrained planning." A note of pride rang in Sir Anthony's voice, and Viola's hand squeezed his convulsively.

"So Selby knew again and again of the plans—and betrayed him," she whispered, her hand to her throat.

"Yes, I fear so. Oh, not at the beginning. Even Giorgio did not trust me, and told me nothing until afterward. Then, laughing like a boy, he would tell me what he had done, the messages he had intercepted. Presently he came to trust me, and I—I betrayed him."

"But not knowingly, Father!" she cried out, pleadingly.

"No, my darling, but that does not excuse me. Giorgio trusted me to tell no one. However, I had the habit of confiding in Selby. He seemed so keen, so interested. He was excellent in handling details. I would confide in him, go over matters with him—and Giorgio's missions began to fail. He was upset, but I consoled him," he said bitterly, his free hand pressed to his forehead. "I told him a man must be prepared for some failures. I cautioned him to be more careful. I—cautioned!"

Viola was silent. She could not console him for a

time. Her heart was bitter for Giorgio, the eager, laughing boy who had died in the wars, never to revive.

"Then—that final mission—"

"Yes," he said. "I told Selby. I have been remembering, as I sat alone in the study, nights when I could not sleep. I have gone over and over the details of those weeks. Giorgio came to me with a daring plan. It was complicated, and I warned him not to try it. He insisted he must get through the lines to carry information to our troops. Before he went, I confided in Reginald Selby—my invaluable aide! We went over the plans, Selby suggested small changes—I agreed, and told Giorgio. He trusted me—oh, God, he trusted me, and did as I said."

"And then—"

"The Doria were waiting. They held him. I did not know it until weeks later, when I had given up waiting for Giorgio to return. They took him away, along with his father and mother and sister. They were all tortured—for days. His sister died first. Then the mother, then the father. And Giorgio, pretending more weakness than he felt, bribed one guard, dove from the window of the castle where he was held, into the shallow waters below, injuring himself, but managing to drag himself and swim somehow—God knows how— He escaped, and hid with some shepherds for weeks, months. I thought he was dead. The message never got through."

"But how did you know about his family?" She forced herself to continue. Oustide, the storm accompanied their talk. She would forever remember the words, with the thunder rolling ominously about them, the slashes of lightning making her flinch.

"Word came to me—" He swallowed, then forced

himself to say the words. "Word came—the bodies of the three had been dumped before the gates of Florence, out on the main road. They were recognized, although— My dear, I cannot go on."

He covered his face with his hands.

"They were buried in the family graveyard," she whispered, repeating what Carmela had said.

"Yes. With honors. Everyone knew then that it was the Doria. I thought they had cunningly traced Giorgio, and captured him. They had fought with the French, dogs that they were. When the wars were over, I returned to England, hoping to forget everything. Yet everyone wondered, and I went over and over in my mind—how could the Doria have traced Giorgio? Now, I know, I betrayed him myself."

"They used you, Father," she said quietly, knowing now why Giorgio had been so terribly bitter. The mission had been their secret, yet he guessed that her father had unwittingly told someone the whole plan. "Did you ever tell Giorgio—"

"No, I did not know for certain. Yet I began to suspect Selby—"

Selby came back into the room, unsteady on his legs, yet his eyes were as fiery as ever. "Come, your bedrooms are ready," he sneered at them.

"My daughter and I remain together," said Sir Anthony calmly.

Selby glared at him, but Sir Anthony would not be moved. Finally he allowed them to go to a dusty bedroom with sheets hastily laid on the beds. Sir Anthony urged Viola to lie down.

"It may be two or three days before—before anyone comes," he said.

She sighed. And when Giorgio came, he would be killed, unless they were very clever and quick. She thought and thought as she lay there, her cloak pulled over her to keep from using the damp, dusty blankets.

She wakened several times in the night. Her father lay on the bed near the doorway, and she thought he must be awake. But they said nothing. A guard paced slowly up and down the hall, paused to drink from his bottle, to grumble to another guard, and pace on.

In the morning she was glad to rise. She was tired, dusty, unrefreshed. Her father was haggard, his face stubbled with gray beard. But he had never looked so dear to her as when he gave her a smile, and murmured, "Courage, my dear. We have not lost yet, and Giorgio is a clever man."

A guard brought a basin of water for them to wash in, then beckoned them curtly to the drawing room. Some attempt had been made to clean it, but dust still lay thickly on the carpets, the window sills, and the mantel, above which lay the rust-edged swords.

Another guard brought them hot coffee and some dry bread and cheese. They ate thankfully, and were courteous to him. He mellowed enough to sit on a chair with the back before him, willing to talk with them and exchange gossip.

His accent was strange; she thought it must be of Pisa. He spoke of the storm, how it still rained and the roads were muddy and some flooded. A bridge was out below them. Lightning had struck a tree on the grounds. He had caught two rabbits, and they would have a fine lunch.

Viola wondered if they might bribe him to let them go. Selby was asleep, snoring audibly in another bedroom. Her father shook his head slightly when she whispered it to him. When the guard took the tray away, Sir Anthony said, "He would take the money and cut our throats. He has no scruples. Do not be deceived."

"But Giorgio will walk into a trap. I am the bait!" Tears came to her eyes, and were forced back with effort.

"He is an intelligent man. Do not worry."

Her father was right. It was futile to worry. She prayed instead, thinking of the tender face of the blue-clad Madonna in the painting Giorgio had given her recently. She had found the family chapel in his villa, and when he learned she wished to pray in it, he had found a precious painting, and had it set up, with blue curtains about it, and before it a prayer stool of carved wood and a kneeling bench of blue velvet. She visited it daily, and found it a tremendous comfort. She wished she were there now, and closed her eyes, bringing up the image of the Madonna before her. "Save Giorgio," she prayed. "Oh, God, he has suffered enough. Save him this time, and let me help if I can, to redeem Father from his shame!"

She felt stronger and quieter when she had prayed, and she opened her eyes to find her father studying her.

"You have matured, my dear," he said. "Giorgio has been good to you and for you."

"I love him," she said simply. "He has been marvelous to me. He is a magnificent man. If only I could help him—"

"And I."

Selby stumbled into the room later, eyes bloodshot and face flushed. He had not bothered to shave or to change his clothing. He snapped at the guards, who answered with sullen impudence.

Then, at noon, they had more visitors. When they heard the sounds of several horses, Viola and her father stiffened in excitement and apprehension.

Selby moved to the door, and waited idly, frowning. When the horses came close, he called out, "Hey, Niccolo, look at the birds I have captured! You said I could not do it!"

Niccolo Leopardo came up the steps of the villa and into the room. When he saw Viola sitting composedly with her father, he cursed. "*Per Dio*! You cannot do anything right! Why did you drag him into this? Do you think to escape, once you have killed an English nobleman?"

Selby shrugged. "Oh, but I shall not kill him," he said, and grinned lazily. "*Signor* Michieli will kill him and his daughter, and in the meantime he will receive wounds which cause his own death. All in this deserted hunting lodge. It is well known now that Sir Anthony betrayed the good *Signor* Michieli. All Florence will mourn them, eh?"

Niccolo Leopardo stared down at them, his face flushed and disturbed. His small black eyes seemed pinpoints in his dark face. He had ridden hard, judging by his muddy riding suit and his weary face. Behind him came three men.

"The Doria," whispered Sir Anthony, and his hand clasped Viola's.

Selby heard him. "Yes, the Doria. I promised them a part in killing Giorgio. They deserve it, eh? Enrico, come in, my friend! This is Enrico Doria, the great head of the family. This is Marco Doria, brother of Enrico. This is Taddeo." And he indicated the bulky form of the man who followed last. Thick, brutish, all of them, with tough, stupid faces, thought Viola. Like animals, and she thought of Giorgio's word for them—wolves.

"You are an idiot," said Niccolo Leopardo, giving

way to rage tinged with fear. "He will not come alone this time! He will be too clever for that."

"Not after the message I left for him. I told him little Viola was spending some nights with me." Selby flung back his head and laughed without mirth. "He will come chasing up here."

"I hope you are right. I'll have no part in it—"

Selby's laughter stopped abruptly. "You are in this with me, my friend," he said with deadly menace. "Do you think to go on living in Florence when I am banished? Oh, no, you share my fate always, remember that!"

Sir Anthony was staring at them both. "So you were in this always, Leopardo?" he asked softly, with grim hate. "And I trusted you also!"

"Oh, you were ever a trusting fool!" said Leopardo with great contempt. "A dupe and fool! Thinking you were so clever because you were British! How I laughed behind your back!"

"*I* am British, and you are a stupid Italian," said Selby, and the men would have come to blows had Enrico Doria, middle-aged, graying, not stepped between them.

"You forget what we come for. We want Michieli. The last of his line," grumbled the older man, shaking his shaggy head.

Someone called out sharply in Italian. The men stiffened. Viola had not caught the words, but she could not mistake their eager, waiting stances, heads forward as though sniffing the blood of the enemy.

A single horse was approaching steadily. Finally the man pulled up and called out. It was Giorgio's clear, ringing voice.

Someone answered him with a growl, and presently the footsteps of booted feet were heard on the villa steps. Viola sat up erectly, her eyes flashing. She dared not look toward the rusty swords above the mantel, but they could be used, they could. Giorgio came into the doorway, and paused a moment to adjust his eyes to the light.

He was dressed entirely in black–black trousers, black boots, black shirt and coat. His dark head was erect. He looked like the nobleman he was, standing beside those horrible men, thought Viola proudly. His dark eyes flicked once at her, took in her posture beside her father, their clasped hands. Then his look went over Sir Anthony, cool and critical. Finally the dark head turned and he gazed at Selby, and at Leopardo, at the three Doria men ranged along the wall behind them.

"So we are all together," sneered Selby. His voice was high-pitched with excitement. He came up to Giorgio and glared at him. "Would you like me to tell you what I have done with your pretty wife?"

"My father-in-law is here, I see," said Giorgio, his voice as cold as the snow on the Alps. "Viola, you are unharmed?"

"Yes, Giorgio, as you see," she said with composure, before anyone could stop her.

"But not for long!" cried Selby. "I shall take her in your presence, what pleasure for me! She will die slowly, by my hand, or that of Taddeo Doria, who did so well by your pretty little sister! You remember that?"

"I remember everything," said Giorgio. He had no pistol in his belt. The man behind him held his dagger, the distinctive, small dagger with the Michieli crest. Yet he dominated them all with his presence.

"I have learned much today," said Viola quietly, as calmly as her husband. She had been thinking, praying, and something had come to her. Giorgio would not have come completely alone. Behind him must be his friends—only a short way behind, she prayed—to help in the trap. Alessandro Peruzzi, and others, they must be there. He would not be so reckless now, as he had been as a boy!

"And what is that?" asked Giorgio, moving one step closer to the mantel, as though merely shifting his weight. She prayed that he had seen the swords, for she dared not glance toward them.

"Father told me what happened during the wars. He was foolish enough to trust his aide, Reginald Selby. He began telling him of your missions, consulting him. He did not mean to betray you, Giorgio."

"Mean it or not, he did betray!" sneered Selby. "He was a fool! He played into my hands!"

Leopardo shifted impatiently. "Why all this talk? We must do the deed quickly, and be away from this cursed place!"

"You are a coward, you do not even enjoy what must be done," Selby said impatiently. His eyes glittered. "I have made my plans, and you must make yours!"

"I have no wish to leave Florence," muttered Leopardo. "Someone will tell eventually."

"Who? We leave no signs, except that Giorgio Michieli has killed his wife and the father-in-law who betrayed him, after discovering his deceit. What could be easier? The bodies will be discovered here one day." Selby sounded so callous that Viola wanted to rage at him. But that was not the way.

Hulking Taddeo Doria moved foward a few steps, impatient with the talking. "Let me have him, let me have him," he grumbled. "I will carve him to pieces slowly. You can watch him die."

"No, I'll have the woman first," Selby answered greedily, going over to Viola, stepping deliberately in front of Giorgio. He yanked her up from the sofa, and pulled her to him. She smelled the sweat on him, the heavy scent he wore, felt the heat of excitement.

She stood rigidly, not permitting him to draw her closer. She kept her eyes on his face. If she could throw him off guard, if Giorgio did not get careless. . . .

She saw Giorgio's furtive move to one of the swords above the mantel. Selby's head began to turn. She put up her hands to hold his cheeks with her palms, and smiled at him deliberately.

"Well, Mr. Selby, you surprise me," she began. "Yes, you do surprise me—"

He was staring at her, caught off guard for a fatal moment. Giorgio leaped—not at Selby, but at Leopardo, who had drawn a dagger.

A sword thrust, a cry, then Leopardo slid slowly from the long blade, crumpling onto the dusty carpet. His eyes were open for a long time, staring upward, the small black eyes bewildered before they went blank. Blood seeped from the narrow wound which had gone deep—deep enough.

Viola tried desperately to hold Selby back. He cursed her and flung her from him. She regained her balance, and saw him leap for Giorgio. Behind them, her father grabbed the second sword from the mantel, and lunged toward Selby.

Enraged, the man turned to him, and engaged him with his dagger. The Doria leaped forward, daggers in hand, wolfish grins on their swarthy faces.

Viola backed from them until the sofa stopped her. The burly brute Taddeo was coming toward her, dagger poised.

She held herself steady. She must be as quick as a cat, she must be—she must . . .

She heard a screech, and Taddeo turned his head sharply. Sir Anthony was thrusting a second time into Selby, backed against a wall, skewered there by the long sword, its rusty blade crimsoned by his blood. He was staring, green eyes glistening, hanging on the sword. Then he fell forward, and the sword went right up through his body and out his back.

The Italian guard at the door was dashing at Giorgio, dagger upraised. He had turned to meet the thrust, and Taddeo was moving toward him. Viola screamed and rushed forward to catch at Taddeo's thick arm. He turned on her, and his dagger caught her shoulder, almost in the same spot where she had been injured before. She felt nothing but the cold bite of steel; she hung on until he shook her from him as though she were a kitten in his path. She fell to the floor from the hard push he had given her.

The Italian guard was down, writhing, clutching at his half-severed right arm. Giorgio turned and, with the Michieli dagger which he had grabbed from the limp hand of the guard, thrust into the body of Taddeo Doria. His face hard-set and cold as death, he thrust again, and again. And finally the hulking brute went down, sprawling over the body of Niccolo Leopardo.

From outside came the sounds of horses and shouts. "Ah—Michieli, we come, we come!"

Enrico Doria and his brother Marco were closing in on Giorgio now. With a sword in his right hand and a dagger in his left, he parried them. Viola was weakening from the loss of blood which spurted from her shoulder. Her eyes were dimming. But Giorgio—Giorgio was still upright, though his face was bleeding from cuts, and his left shoulder showed a great rent. Then Alessandro Peruzzi and several other men charged into the room.

Viola managed to prop herself up with her father's help. She clung to him wide-eyed as the men fought. Grim-faced, mouths tight-clamped, they fought with swords and daggers until Enrico Doria flung up one arm and cried, in Italian so thick she scarcely understood, "I surrender. Peace, in the name of God—peace—"

His left arm was severed at the shoulder. Viola shuddered and turned away her gaze. Sir Anthony held her against his shoulder, anxiously trying to staunch the blood that flowed from it. Marco Doria, bleeding from a dozen wounds, sullenly echoed his brother's words. "Peace—in the name of God—peace—"

"Let them be," said Giorgio, finally lowering his sword and dagger. "Let them—be—" He went over to Viola as the other men began disarming the Italian guards and the Doria who remained alive. Taddeo Doria hung limp over the body of Leopardo. Selby lay in a pool of blood, his handsome face blank in death.

Giorgio knelt by Viola. "Poor child, you are hurt—yet again." She tried to smile at his anxious face, but to her shame she fainted, and fell back into her father's arms.

CHAPTER 15

It was October before Viola left her bed for more than a few minutes at a time. She was impatient at her own weakness, for Giorgio had not remained in his bed. He had been up, his arm in a sling, going about his work. But still she lay in enforced quiet in her bedroom.

Finally the doctor allowed her to sit up for part of the day on her lounge. The weather had turned cool, and only in the midafternoon was it warm enough for her to sit on her balcony.

Then her friends were allowed to come, and her sisters. Sir Anthony had already made a habit of coming every few days, and Viola's heart had been glad at the new friendship and closeness between herself and her father, between her father and Giorgio. All was forgiven.

Lucia Peruzzi came first, imperiously claiming it as her right to visit her dear friend. Viola welcomed her with open arms, and there were tears in the eyes of the countess as she bent and kissed Viola. "Dearest friend, how I have grieved for you! You are much better, now, yes?"

"Oh, yes. I am so angry that they make me stay so quiet! I am quite well again."

Lucia patted her cheek affectionately, and settled her skirts about her as she seated herself on a chair beside the chaise. "Be at ease. I shall tell you all the fresh gossip of Florence, and relate everything that has gone on. Of course, you must know that all are singing the praises of your so courageous husband, and your Papa!"

"Oh, tell me about it," urged Viola shamelessly, and Lucia laughed and complied.

Everyone in Tuscany was excited that the truth had been uncovered. Giorgio had carried out many dangerous missions, with the help of Sir Anthony. His courage was so magnificent that one must make up ballads about him, and Lucia proceeded to sing one of the more modest ones. She omitted the verses about the cursed Doria, merely explaining that they contained some words Viola would not wish to hear.

As for Reginald Selby, and that horrible villain to his people, Niccolo Leopardo, their bodies had been burned, and the ashes scattered on a dung heap. Viola shuddered at that, closing her eyes. Taddeo Doria's body had been returned to Pisa, and his people had buried him quietly. It was hoped that without his brutal strength to back them, his brothers would choose the peace they had pleaded for.

Giorgio came up to her drawing room presently, with Alessandro Peruzzi close behind him. The count bent over Viola's hand ceremoniously, and she beamed up at him.

"You are recovering. How glad we are. But this

must not continue, dear little Viola! Every time, you bear the worst of your husband's scrapes!"

She laughed, and Lucia laughed also, giving Giorgio a teasing look. "No, no, I have had enough of being injured!" Viola assured him. "We are going to remain at home and keep well away from trouble, are we not, Giorgio?"

"You may be sure of it," he said sternly.

Viola squeezed Alessandro's hand warmly. "And may I thank you, sir, for—"

"For what? I did only what a man of honor must," he said, reddening with embarrassment. She had learned he had fought like a madman against all those who attacked Giorgio and herself.

"For being such a good friend of Giorgio's, and I hope of mine," she said simply, smiling radiantly at him.

He kissed the hand he still held, and smiled back at her, his stern face softening. "But the friends of a man are a credit to himself, and reflect honor on him, *ma donna*," he said.

She was weary when they left, and slept for a time, and Giorgio cursed with some of his old temper, and said there would be no more company for a while.

But in another week, she received her father and her sisters, who had been begging to come to her. Eleanor and Bernice were charming, and much sobered by their sister's and father's experiences.

"I did not wholly trust Reginald Selby, yet he was so chivalrous to me," Eleanor confided. "Dear God, what if I had married him?" She shuddered, her face quite pale.

Bernice hugged her older sister reassuringly. "There, darling, you have wept enough. Do not again, I beg you, you will only disturb dear Viola, who has borne enough! Papa says we shall soon return to England, and there we shall cheer up. If only Viola would come with us for a time!"

Viola shook her blond curls. "I shall never leave Giorgio. If you wish my company, you must come to Florence!"

Sir Anthony came up presently with Giorgio. He studied Viola's face. "More color, I think. By Jove, you look blooming, my dear."

"Thank you, Father. You are in good spirits, I think?"

He sat down with his customary elegance. Yet she never looked at him now without remembering how he had comforted her that horrible night, how he had fought like a tiger for her. Behind the smooth diplomat was a man of sensibility and integrity, and she was profoundly grateful to him, and ashamed that she had ever doubted him.

He soon told them the reason for his good spirits. "With the good will of your husband and of Count Peruzzi, my mission is accomplished. The final draft of the trade agreement has been written out. It only remains for the formal signatures to be added, and I may return to England and to private life."

"Oh, Papa, how splendid," said Viola weakly. She looked up at Giorgio, who bent over her to make sure she was well covered against a draft from the open French windows. Outside, the last petals of the crimson roses were drooping against the balcony railing. In the gardens below, the flower beds were brilliant with scarlet salvia, crimson and orange gladioli, yellow marigolds—the bright heralds of autumn.

Giorgio nodded. "All difficulties have been resolved, little one," he said quietly. And she knew, meeting his eyes, that his last bitterness against her father had dissolved.

"If only I had not been such a trusting fool," Sir Anthony burst out angrily. "I condemn myself! Never again will I go into such secret missions, I could not trust myself!"

"You do yourself wrong," said Giorgio with composure. "But tell me—those details of my last mission, those changes, were they your ideas?"

"No, Selby's. I presented them as my own."

"And I trusted you completely. As I do again," said Giorgio quickly, as a dull flush filled the older man's face. "Now let us forget all that. It is the past, and I much prefer the present, and my new happiness."

They talked then of other matters, of the return to England. "But you must persuade Giorgio to bring you to England, since you will not come with us!" Sir Anthony urged Viola. "A good long visit, a court presentation. We shall arrange all."

"Perhaps one day," she smiled. "When Giorgio has the time and the wish to travel."

"I shall need your help in choosing husbands for Eleanor and Bernice," said Sir Anthony. "You have done so well for yourself that I think your judgment must be impeccable! Eh? Will you come for that?"

"Really, Father, I shall do my own choosing," snapped Eleanor, scowling her displeasure.

"You have not done as well as your sister," Sir Anthony replied blandly, and gave Viola a little wink.

"We might come in a year or so, sir," Giorgio said. "As you suggest, Viola has good judgment. When your sisters are thinking of wedding, Viola, we shall go to them, shall we not? For they must be as happy in their marriage as we are." His tone was gentle.

"Of course you must come," said Bernice blithely,

no longer afraid of him. "After all, you are our only brother! If I should choose as badly as Eleanor did, you must be sure to tell me!" And she laughed wickedly at the outraged expression on Eleanor's face.

All laughed except Eleanor, and she finally, graciously allowed herself to be teased and charmed into good humor again. They departed with the promise that someday Viola and Giorgio would come to England for a good long visit.

Giorgio came upstairs again after the guests had left. Viola was lying back on her chaise, gazing out contentedly at the glorious orange and red streaks of the sunset over Florence. The bells were beginning to chime, far below them in the valley.

"You are not too weary, my dear?" he said at once.

She reached out her hand for his, and he came and sat beside her on the couch. "Would you really like to go to England with me?" she murmured. "I should like so much to show you the London I discovered for myself, in walks with my chaperone. And the country, where our home was, with golden oaks and dense thickets, and our riding stables."

He bent and kissed her cheek gently. "I shall plan on it, my darling. I want to know all about your earlier years, so that I may plan how to exceed your happiness in them! I want you to be the happiest woman in the world."

She curled her palm against his cheek. "But I am most happy now, Giorgio, you know that."

"But do you prefer to be in society? Would you like to join the court? It could be done," he said, with some reserve, his hand going to her hand, and pressing it to his cheek. She knew he was thinking of his scar, how people would stare and whisper.

"No, I should not like it," she said. "I wish to be

alone with you. Oh, it is quite pleasant to hear people sing your praises, but when Lucia speaks of a bright season, and many parties—oh, Giorgio, I do prefer to be here with you." She was flushed; it had cost her an effort to say this.

"Ah, yes, they talk too much, and gush on about heroes," he said with a frown. "It is displeasing. I would rather be left in peace."

"That is what I like also," she added musingly, "though I do like Lucia. And how sweet it was of old Countess Alberti to come all the way to us the other day. It was such an effort for her. We shall repay the visit one day, I promised her."

"*Si*, we shall." He was silent for a time. "Viola, do you recall how we met?"

She turned her head from contemplation of the dusky gardens, and looked at him in surprise. "Recall? Of course I do."

"You looked so lovely with the violets in your hand. But my heart was hardened to beauty. I would not admit that a girl could be gentle and compassionate enough to accept me of her own will. Then I saw you in your home, how your sisters—thoughtlessly, I am sure—pushed you into doing all the work, while denying you the privileges they took for granted. All that work, and no pleasure!"

"Oh, but that is all past—they did not mean—" She was quite startled by the seriousness of his tone, the way he sat back from her and studied her keenly.

"I did not expect to live long," he said after a time.

She put her hand to her mouth, suppressing a cry. She gazed at him, her eyes wide.

"Yes, it is true. I knew in my heart that Leopardo was my enemy, though I had no real evidence of it. Then Selby returned also, and always they had their heads together. I then learned that the Doria had been active, and finally they were seen in Florence. Somehow my soul was dead in me, and I did not care enough to continue fighting for myself. What use? I had no family, no parents, no sisters—no—no son."

"Oh, I thought that—" she whispered. He heard, and curled his hand about her fingers, leaning to her once more, his dark eyes earnest.

"Forgive me for what I did to you, Viola. I spoke of revenge, yet I thought only of your gallantry, the way you pretended not to care when everyone went off in beautiful dresses to the dinner and the balls. I thought to leave the money to you, so you would be comfortable and free of your demanding, unloving family. I saw only the surface, not the deep love your father had for you, and your sisters. And so I took your youth, your sweetness, and dragged you from the future you might have had with them."

Her lips moved dryly, she could not utter a syllable. He did not love her, he regretted marrying her, he had no true affection for her! Perhaps he wished to marry some Italian girl—and a spasm of hatred blazed in her for that horrible woman who might claim him!

Giorgio went on, gazing anxiously into her white face. "Perhaps I should not speak of it now, you are still so weak, and now you are pale and languid. But I feel my heart is full, and I must attempt to express—forgive me, Viola. I must tell you of my growing love for you. Your disregard of my—horrible face—this scar—how you welcomed me to your bed—it softened me from a hardness in my soul, which I had thought dead to all love and gentleness. Gradually I changed, and it was you who accomplished it.

"I wanted you to be comfortable, free of your family," he went on musingly. "Instead, because of me, you were attacked, constantly in danger. I was frantic. This lovely girl, so innocent and good, was in danger of death because of me! How could I have done this to you! I still blame myself bitterly."

"I—did it to myself," she said dully. "I agreed to the marriage—"

"Because you loved your father, and thought to repair his shame! But there was no shame. And my revenge crumbled to dust in my hands. Viola, can you forgive me? I have learned to love you with my whole soul. But if you wish to leave me, make a new life, return to England that you love so much—"

She seemed to come alive, as though spring had bloomed after a long winter. "Giorgio—you—love me?" she whispered.

"Yes, have I not told you so?" he said, surprised, his face grave and anxious. "You must know—from the way I embraced you, how I need you, how you have changed me. You know that I love you with all my heart and soul. You are my hope for eternity—"

"Oh, Giorgio!" She wavered between laughter and tears. Did man ever blunder so much? Did woman ever so misunderstand? What had seemed so clear and simple to him had caused her such anguish! One day when they were closer she might scold him for this. Now she thought only to reassure him. "I have come to love you also, so very much. Why else did I—welcome you to my bed?" She knew she was blushing furiously, but perhaps he would blame the scarlet of the sunset reflected on her face. "I came to respect you, to honor you, then to love and adore you with all that I am. I never want to leave you. It would be to die. Oh, Giorgio—"

He bent closer to gaze in her face in the darkening dusk of the room. "Can I believe it?" he marveled, his tone light. "Did you love me then, when you welcomed me so sweetly? I could not believe that night! You yielded to my every caress as though you desired it. I thought you pretended, because you wished to do your duty. But all thoughts of duty were swept from my brain when you responded to me, caressed my face, my ugly face—"

"Your handsome face!" She pressed her hands to his cheeks lovingly. "Do you know you have a profile like those on Roman coins? You are the handsomest man in the world!"

"Now I am convinced that you love me, you would not be so blind—" His laughter choked on tears, and he bent his lips to her throat, to the curve of her shoulder. She stroked his thick, dark hair, rejoicing in his love for her, in hers for him.

"And I drew you into danger," he muttered again. "Your loveliness—your faith—and I could not keep you safe."

She smiled a little wisely above his dark head. "Oh, my darling, *mio caro*, I do not expect safety," she assured him strongly. "But I do want love! All you can give me—for I am starved for it."

He lifted his head to gaze down at her, slipping his arms about her slim form, caressing her with his hands. "Oh, *carissima, amoretta,* how I shall love you!" he promised. "You shall have all the love you can carry, in full measure. For all of my love is yours, and I am in danger of hurting you with my desire for you."

"You have never hurt me," she whispered. "I adore you, I want you—*amore mio*—"

How he kissed her then, his lips clinging passionately to her warm lips. But always he was gentle. And she knew that no matter what he said, she was safe in his hands; he loved her as she had so desired to be loved. With passion that was yet gentle, with desire that was yet sweet, with strength and toughness to protect her, and never to hurt.

She was safe in his arms, where she had longed to be.

IN 1918 AMERICA FACED AN ENERGY CRISIS

An icy winter gripped the nation. Frozen harbors blocked the movement of coal. Businesses and factories closed. Homes went without heat. Prices skyrocketed. It was America's first energy crisis now long since forgotten, like the winter of '76-'77 and the oil embargo of '73-'74. Unfortunately, forgetting a crisis doesn't solve the problems that cause it. Today, the country is relying too heavily on foreign oil. That reliance is costing us over $40 billion dollars a year Unless we conserve, the world will soon run out of oil, if we don't run out of money first. So the crises of the past may be forgotten, but the energy problems of today and tomorrow remain to be solved. The best solution is the simplest conservation. It's something every American can do.

ENERGY CONSERVATION -

IT'S YOUR CHANCE TO SAVE, AMERICA

Department of Energy, Washington, D.C

A PUBLIC SERVICE MESSAGE FROM DELL PUBLISHING CO., INC.